A RING OF OAK & APPLE

EOIN BRADY

EOINBRADYBOOKS.COM

1

THE RINGFORT

Silence was harder to deal with than the weeping. Periods of calm and quiet were cruel. They allowed the mind to wallow in the memory of what survival cost. It never lasted long though, weepers were always close. Fin was almost thankful for the numbing cold. It was far easier to deal with the threat of exposure than to try and cope with insurmountable guilt. The mind needed to be occupied to keep out the ghosts. When it was too dangerous to toil and travel, pain worked as an adequate substitute.

Right now he needed to get off the river and find somewhere to rest. A few bottles of whiskey rolled around the bottom of the kayak. They would keep the nightmares at bay. He considered continuing on through the night. There would be a bright, full moon to light his path. It was tempting to let the current take him through Ireland, but he was already going on two days without sleep. It dulled his reactions. Only a matter of time before that killed him.

Fin was on the water for so long that he was not sure that it was still the same river. He had lost track of what day it was weeks ago. Nights and, when necessary, days were spent in abandoned homes. The last time he stopped he was trapped and killed time by painting the kayak a dark brown with house paint. He had hoped to mask the vivid red plastic of his craft in an attempt to draw less attention, but the infestation of weepers had not given him long enough for the paint to dry. *Did they smell the fumes?* The paint washed away in the river and the rain.

How do they keep finding me? Fin rested the paddle on the kayak and traced his fingers across the surface of the river. He scooped up a handful of water and splashed his face. "They're not following you. Start thinking like that, you'll go mad." It had been so long since he last spoke that his voice rasped. The dead had harassed him ceaselessly since the beginning of the outbreak that devoured Ireland. He hoped it was just his exhausted mind that gave the infected more wits than they actually had.

The water was black and dotted with small whirling pools that twirled across the surface, hinting at turbulent currents below. The eroded bank to his left was high and earthy, bored by rats or migrant birds. Heavy rainfall had transformed every timid tributary into an agitated, pulsing rapid. Fin was little more than a novice in the kayak. If the river rose any higher or became any fiercer, he would be forced to land. Desperation, and a determination to never allow himself become trapped again, was all that kept him going .

The field to his right was low enough for him to see the leafless hedges at its perimeter. The grass was dark and lush, almost impervious to the winter ice. Come morning it would be beautiful, glistening in a cloak of frost. *I will not survive another night out in the open.* Before the outbreak, Fin had thought of himself as being overweight. Now he was trimmer than he had ever been in his adult life. He could put a finger between his ribs. *Wouldn't mind a bit of pudge on my bones now.*

The severe cold did not kill the infected as he had so desperately hoped it would. It hastened the weepers' transformation into zombies, but at least the weepers had the decency to announce they were going to kill you. They wept and wailed when they spotted prey. The zombies were silent. They lacked the speed and mobility of weepers, but often you did not know you were being watched by a zombie until they had their teeth in you. He was almost convinced that they sought shelter in buildings during the coldest nights. At this point in the quarantine most of the houses he entered were barren. Survivors were like locusts, leaving little behind. Some homes were burial mounds now. Shrines to those that were either too afraid to leave, or chose to die with some dignity, rather than face a gruesome end or the protracted loss of their humanity.

It feels like a Monday. It was the strangest things that got on Fin's nerves; for instance, he spent an inordinate amount of time trying to figure out what day of the week it was. *Every day feels like a Monday.* He could make a guess at the month by the small stretch coming into the evening. The sun would linger a little longer, but it still felt like he barely made any ground with the extra time. The night was going to be cloudless, he knew what little heat there was would flee the world the moment the sun set. Pushing on was stupid, but moving was probably his only way to keep warm.

Fin was cautious by nature; he had survived this long because he tested every possible failing of a choice before actually making it. He kept to fields and countryside, skirting along hedgerows instead of walking in the open. The journey across Ireland was going to take months. If by some miracle his loved ones were not already dead, they would be by the time he reached them. The river then was his only option for relative safety and speed. The only drawback really was that he was likely going to drown. The kayak had already turned a few times and tossed him into the freezing river, often over churning weirs.

He shuddered at the thought of it happening in the dark. Or getting caught in the knitting of roots that wove across the riverbed. *Your bones might make it home, eventually.* Storm clouds had passed him earlier in the day. He had been on edge for hours, waiting for the rush and swell of a rain-engorged river.

Most of the fields he passed were divided either by fences, hedges, walls or roads. If any of the infected were following him, they could not possibly keep pace. Fin wondered why he had not encountered many people on the river. At night he caught the slow light of satellites streaking across the shadow of Ireland. By day there were no more aeroplanes in the sky, no contrails to trace back and wonder after their origin.

Whenever he came across livestock, they ran to him full of excitement and questions he could not hope to answer. Those occasions he would stop to break down fences for them or cut through wires. Giving them more pasture to roam. Some paddocks were so packed with cattle or sheep that they had starved themselves. It was an unlucky time of year for the world to end, most farm animals were housed in sheds. Those were full of rotten flesh and skin too big for bones.

He was exhausted, full of doubt and fear, and he faced an enemy that never questioned itself and never slept. All that drove them was a need to feed or infect. Against such a creature, Fin knew he had already lost. Stress was a constant vice gripping his chest. *But you're still breathing.* Some people he encountered had lost patches of hair from worry. Others broke out in hives. They were the lucky ones – others lost their minds. He kept moving, only just keeping ahead of bad memories and malignant thoughts. *Not much sanity to what I'm doing.* Drink helped, specifically spirits, whiskey, but he no longer had a preference. The goal was brief oblivion. Hangovers were a nice distraction in the mornings too.

The meandering bends in the river had been uneventful, calm had coddled his wits. What he had assumed was a tree stump moved. Fin was too close to hide. He turned the paddle blade in the water to slow down and manoeuvre into deeper water. The river burbled and for a moment he thought the kayak would upend.

What had once been a man stared into the river, then walked off the bank, disappearing with an insignificant splash. If it struggled, it lost against the deep and cruel currents. It did not rise.

Fin paddled close to the opposite bank to catch his breath. He remained hidden in the long reeds, waiting to hear the weeping of nearby infected riled by the noise. *Was it a weeper, or was that suicide? Should I have said something?* He imagined a starving person filling their pockets with stones and stepping off the bank. *Was it an infected lured by its own reflection?* Fin often wondered what went through their heads before they died. To walk and run required significant brain function. The small hairs across his body stood on end. He pushed off from the bank, entering the swifter flow of water. There was no point stopping here. He doubted he would find anything other than last letters filled with regrets.

* * *

The setting sun cast long shadows ahead of him. There was still beauty in the world and he tried not to be numb to it. He realised, though, that he just used it as another distraction from the thoughts that plagued him. The dappled last light of day could not stop his mind from picking moments apart. Gallows humour helped, just not when you were alone. The man that went into the river unsettled him for the rest of the day. *The infection is always fatal. Maybe he was bitten. Instead of turning into one of those creatures, he decided to end it.* Fin paddled faster than was wise, to banish the image of a body being buffeted by the deafening thrum of the river. *Will he turn down there? Will he wash up and roam the countryside as a zombie?* Despite everything, that word still gave him trouble. *It's ridiculous. Once this is over, they'll have to come up with a more serious name for them. If this ever ends.*

The infected did not become faster during the night, nor did their numbers grow, but the dark was the canvas for Fin's black thoughts. There were more screams during the night, he was almost certain of it. His theory was that survivors lost so much hope, that they often forgot that the sun would eventually rise. Those screams were his only contact with others. You learned to read the different types. There were guttural and brief ones. Those meant the person was likely dead or dying. Then there were those long and horrible ones, filled with despair. Those ones could overwhelm you if you were not careful. Fin hated the sound even more than the weeping and the silence. They filled the night with a horrible, infectious mania. Sharing a crazed hatred from the lonely and the desperate. The weepers always picked up the call. *Maybe it's a way to not feel so alone.*

Darkness got to people, and he dreaded it. A few times when drink had made his caution impotent, he had to bite his sleeve to stop from screaming himself. Silence was anticipation, a cruel patch of calm in an endless storm, much like the rills and twirls on the river. It was a memory of something that once was. Silence would never be the same again for him. Before the outbreak, the peacefulness along the river would have halved his heart rate. Now it curdled his stomach. What little food he had managed to eat threatened to come back up.

Fin reached into a pocket in the kayak and picked up his toothbrush. The bristles were worn and frayed from overuse. His gums bled often and pained him. He was not sure when he had started brushing his teeth excessively, but it was likely around the time he realised that there were no more dentists. After he had scrubbed his teeth, he brought out a small, nearly empty bottle of perfume. He held the cap to his nose and breathed in the smell of his girlfriend. *Solene.* He searched every house he broke into to find a replacement for his dwindling supply, but he had yet to come across one. Her familiar presence brought his panicked breathing down and slowed his racing thoughts from a gallop to a trot.

Each small comfort brought its own pain. This one made him wonder how Solene was managing. *She could be long dead for all I know.* To banish the thought, he sprayed the smallest amount onto the inside of his dirty mask. He put the bottle away and revelled in her smell. *She's not dead. She's watching the same moon rise.*

* * *

Fin could not settle on a place to land. When the sky was tinged pink and red, he came close to the shallows of a field, but lowing cows caused him to return to the river. If the animals were still alive it meant that there were strong fences or walls around them, but it was likely that they had drawn a crowd of infected.

When there was only a purple hue left in remembrance of the day, panic started to settle in and no amount of perfume could calm him. It was too late now to try to break into a house. He would have to ensure the area was clear first and then go from room to room checking. Once he was alone, he would have to create some form of barrier against the dead. There was the possibility of farm buildings or sheds, or even sleeping out in the open. He knew he would not be able to close his eyes in such situations. Listening to the wildlife and the prospect of an infected just walking onto him would ensure his nerves fizzled away to nothing.

The river slowed before emptying into a large lake. Open space reduced the tightness in his chest. It was a relief compared to the cramped hills and watching woods of the valley. He bit back tears at the brief sensation of triumph at having escaped. In dreams he would return to the slow, shallow, bendy stretches of the ancient waterway. Hear the scratch of riverstones against the underside of the kayak. The weep of excited infected and their churning wake as they trudged towards him. The river was a mass grave from source to sea, but it was the only reason he was still alive. To cross the country by land was suicide.

He let the current and his thoughts carry him far from shore. The wind was sharp and cut with frost. There was light enough to make out the silhouettes of small islands dotted across the lake. The night was clear of weeping, and he could almost fool himself into imagining that the world was back to normal.

He set out for the closest island; the prospect of resting surrounded by a large body of frigid water was the closest to content he had been in a long while. He had a small tent, a dry blanket and a couple of days' worth of sleep to catch up on.

Unusual sounds made him stop and sit low. *People?* He could make out several voices. The undead were not the only ones to be feared, the living still had cunning, wits and hunger. *If they're still talking then they've not seen me yet.* Anger blossomed as a lump in his throat. He wanted so much to be near others, but recent experiences made the hairs stand up on the back of his neck. He paddled away from the island, thinking to find the exit river and continue on. He knew he could not, it was too dark for that now. He needed to consult a map and find some road signs to orient by. *Going on will not save time, I'll lose ground getting lost.*

He listened to the voices. They were too far away to make out words. He only had their tones to judge them by. Conversation was hushed and relaxed. The sound was so sweet and soothing that, despite his better judgement, he followed it like a fish to a lure. He dragged the paddle blades through the water, making no noise. This was exactly what he feared, being in their position, observed, studied, caught unawares. Paranoia set in long ago. It was hard to trust people, especially when you yourself had done some inexcusable things. Things that made him feel like he was closer to being somebody entirely different, so far from his former self that he knew there was not enough forgiveness in the world to return to who he once was.

A dim, warm light shone through thick trees on the largest island. Confident that he was hidden in darkness, Fin approached, silent as a shadow. He waited there and listened, trying to picture faces to match voices. There was good-spirited laughter. *How long has it been since I heard somebody laugh?* He discounted those occurrences when the people involved had gone mad. To him this distant contact was as nourishing as sleep. He just wanted to listen a little longer before leaving.

He waited idle for so long that the cold had made it through his layers and chilled his sweat-dampened tee-shirt. The wind pushed him so far along the shore that he nearly passed the island.

"Have you made up your mind yet?"

Startled, Fin nearly dropped the paddle. Instinctively, he reached for his hammer. He could not see the person who spoke and they did not step out from the tree cover.

"Are you going to stay out there all night long?"

Male. "It's no longer just rude to arrive unannounced. It's dangerous too," Fin said, desperately trying to catch sight of the man.

"Nobody here will think any less of you for showing up without a bottle of wine."

Despite his trepidation, Fin laughed. The sound must have been enough reassurance because the man revealed himself. "We're all strangers here, you're as welcome as anyone else. We just need to check for bites, if you intend on staying until morning. Have you your own food to keep you?"

"A little to share too. Aren't you going to ask me if I'm alone?"

The man motioned for Fin to follow and started walking slowly along the shore. He sighed. "It's a fair question. But what good would come of asking? Say you lied to me to make me think twice about robbing you, I'd lie in your position. Not a good foot to start on. You're worried that if I think you're alone, I might be less inclined to be friendly. It's a loaded question. How horrible does it sound coming from me? Are you alone? I'd piss in my pants if our roles were reversed. I simply don't care if you have more people. To be honest, we could use more. Besides, I watch the shore, I don't need to ask if you're alone."

"For somebody that just said they didn't want to put me on edge, I'm not sure how good of a job you're doing."

The man chuckled. "Where are you coming from?"

"Westport."

The man faltered and slowed. "You know what happened there?"

Fin berated himself for mentioning it, but if the intentions of the people here were bad, at least their curiosity would keep them pleasant for a while. "I do."

"There are some here that would happily give what little they have to speak with you."

"I'm not here to take anything. News for news. We've all lost people and I don't like reminding strangers of that, but if I can give them something, I will," Fin said. "By the way, I heard your camp nearly from the shore. Sound travels far here. If you don't want to be heard, you might be wary of that in the future."

"We wanted to be heard by the living. Personally, I'd keep to a whisper at all times, but if we did that, then there would only be a third of the people here that there are now. You would have paddled right by us and straight into harm. I know I'd be dead if they had not lit the fire the night I passed."

"Harm ahead, what am I in for?"

"I was in Dublin when this started. There are people here from every corner of the country. Some are on the fence about leaving. If you stay, there's a lot of work here to be done, after you're rested of course."

"If I stay? You have it that good here?" Fin asked.

"Compared to what's ahead, yes. I don't think I'll ever

leave this valley again." The man motioned for Fin to paddle towards the shore.

Fin let his momentum carry him in so he could hold the paddle as a weapon, should the need arise. He was too tired to continue, too weary to find somewhere else to lie down and worry until exhaustion closed his eyes or the sun rose. He did not think he could sleep here amongst strangers, but it was his only option. The chance to get information about the route ahead was too tempting to pass up.

The man walked down to the water's edge just as the kayak scraped against the shore. Fin stepped out quickly, uncomfortable being at such a disadvantage. The water in the shallows soaked through his boots and pricked at his skin like shards of ice. "I was just thinking that once I tell the people here about what's chasing me, I doubt they'll want to continue on."

"We're trapped on all sides. I won't shake your hand and I'm not fond of bowing to say hello. I'm Ian."

"Well you didn't attack me the moment I set foot on the island, consider me warmly welcomed."

Ian bent to pick up the back of the kayak. Fin was forced to take the front and lead the way to the camp. "Straight through the trees, you can't miss it."

"I'm Fin. How did yous end up out here?"

"Same as you, drifted on the river. Except we haven't found a good enough reason to leave yet. There's a lot of broken people here. I don't know if there are many whole families left. Some have given up hope of finding loved ones, so they just wait here for things to settle down."

Fin's arms shook, weak from wear. There was no way Ian did not feel it. He shouldered more than his share of the weight and did not complain.

The path to the camp was well-worn. Silver shedding

A Ring of Oak & Apple

birch trees gave way to ancient knotted trunks, bearded with lichen and old moss. Bald from winter. Fin noticed the tiny buds that would unfurl into new leaves in a few weeks. "You don't know what day it is, do you?"

Ian was silent for a moment. "No actually. I haven't thought about that for a long time. Didn't see the point. It's nearly spring though."

The island was littered with old treated stone. Fin could feel a gentle rise beneath his feet. He was not expecting to walk into a ringfort, surrounded by ancient oak and apple trees. Their bare branches scraped the sky, trying to reach for the bulging moon. At its centre, there was a large fire. The walls of the fort kept most of the light hidden from the shore. The trees dispersed the rest. Conversation died down as Fin entered. It was much larger than he expected. Ian walked them into a clearing. Warm shivering light from the fire made the shadows jittery. Tents huddled together. The smell of roasting meat made Fin salivate.

Bags of coal and mounds of turf were hidden from the rain beneath old tarpaulins. By the look of it, these people had settled down for the long haul. Plastic tarps tied to trees funnelled rainwater into barrels.

Fin counted sixteen people in all. A young couple stood a little bit apart from everybody else, they looked ill at ease. Fin assumed they arrived not long before he did by the way they still wore their packs.

Ian helped him carry the kayak close to the fire. "You can rest here tonight. Get some heat into you, you look half dead." He nodded and left without a word of introduction on Fin's behalf.

Fin smiled, but before he could say anything a woman walked up to him and winked. "Strip for us."

Somebody whistled, which got a few sly laughs from the

gathering. There was no embarrassment to the act. Fin undressed while the prying eyes of strangers inspected him for bites and scratches.

The tentative chatter that was slowly returning died away when they saw the bruises and scars on his withered body. Somebody approached him with a sympathetic can of beer. Fin laughed. "Do I look that bad that you're willing to offer me a drink?"

"If you weren't standing I'd suggest a closed casket for the wake," a woman said.

Fin reached into his kayak. The movement made most of the strangers reach for their weapons. "Sorry," he said, as he slowly brought out a bottle of whiskey. "Anyone like a drink?"

2

WHERE WERE YOU WHEN THE WORLD ENDED?

The heat of the fire chipped away at Fin's thawing hands. Swollen fingers responded slowly. Only near the heat was he conscious of how cold the night had become. Before morning, moonlight would reflect off thin ice fringing the slower courses of the river.

He disinfected the can of beer before cracking it open. Bubbles frothed up and spilled over the edge. A lump formed in his throat. He swallowed it down with most of the beer.

Somebody draped a blanket around him. *I hope they didn't notice me flinching.* People settled down around the fire. Fin was the centre of attention. He put the can aside knowing it would not take much to soften his suspicion with so little food in his system.

He rummaged through his store at the bottom of the kayak and took out some tins of food to share. *Better they think of me as an asset rather than a drain on their supplies.*

"It's not pay to stay," the woman who had told him to strip said, though she still took the food without hesitation.

"I'm not paying, I'm pitching in." Fin's lips cracked, he

could taste copper when he ran his tongue across them. He moved a little closer to the fire. "How long have you been here?"

Somebody handed him a bowl of meaty stew. He buried his nose into the rising steam. "I never thought food would bring me to tears, but this does smell good."

"Good stock and spices left here. Most of what you see was left behind by those that lived here before us. They must've been locals. Nobody has come back to try and claim it," somebody said.

Try and claim it. Fin burned the roof of his mouth on the first bite. "They just left this?"

The woman sitting next to him spoke. "I was the first one to arrive. Desperation forced me into the water and I thought I'd drowned and gone to some shitty heaven when I found this. I lit the fire and waited for days for the weepers on the shore to lose interest. Maybe the weepers scared the people off. Or they saw me on the island and didn't want to chance an encounter. I don't know and I don't want to guess because odds are they're dead. I'm Eilish by the way. You met Ian, he mostly just walks the shore, keeping an eye out for new islanders."

Fin nodded his hello.

"Jack is the one that gave you the can of beer and became your best friend when you took out the whiskey," Eilish said.

People started introducing themselves. *Too many.*

"As bad as the weepers are, I was more freaked out by the abandoned camp," Eilish said. "There were photographs and valuables buried among the clothes and at the bottom of sleeping bags. It looked like no more than a heavy rain had upset the tents. There's at least two winters worth of turf and coal for the fires. They must have had large ships to transport everything here, but the only ones left on the lake are small rowing boats. Half of them are barely fit to be taken into deep water. I stayed here and waited, but so far everybody here came from elsewhere."

"Maybe they heard news of a better place and went down the river," Fin said.

"There are no better places," Jack said. "My guess is they brought the infection here with them. If they became weepers, they could have walked into the lake chasing after birds."

"How are you supporting so many people? I'm not asking for specifics. Keep your secrets. I'm curious because most of the houses I've been to have been emptied of food."

"There's excellent farmland in this valley," one of the older men said. "So far we've found a few fields with livestock still in good health. We don't know how to keep the meat if we butcher them, so we're feeding them. If nothing else, they keep most of the infected away from the lake. There's a massive shed stacked so high with boxes of potatoes that you'd need a forklift to reach the ones at the top. One of them could support us for a month."

"A lot of good that will do us," Eilish said. "They'll turn at the end of the season, then we'll have nothing but rot."

"You could always plant them," Fin said.

Nobody was quick to answer. People drank to fill the silence, or just stared into the fire. He knew how they felt. Nobody wanted to believe that this would go on so long that future-proofing now involved farming. *How far will we fall?*

"We've spoken about it," Eilish said. "There's enough equipment and we know where we can find diesel for the tractors, but we'd bring a lot of unwanted attention down on us. Imagine we went to the bother of doing all of that work, only to be swarmed by a horde. We might seem like a large group to somebody used to being alone, but there's a lot to do. Too much. We'd need to set up fences so our fields won't be trampled."

"I don't even think it's just that," Jack said. "The idea of planting in order to eat in a few months, that does something to your mind. I know I find myself thinking that this'll be over in a month. Two, tops. If we put the effort in, the reality hits you that this is the new normal. All you want to do is hide. Not push your boundaries out and fight back against the weepers."

"Stop that talk," a shrill woman said. "We've enough food to keep us going until we're rescued." Her eyes were puffy and red; Fin wondered if her agitation was because of his presence.

Jack gave Fin a sardonic grin. "See what I mean? So, where were you when the world ended?"

Fin chewed the meat in his stew while he thought how best to answer. "Where was I when the world ended?" He smiled. "Hardly dinner talk, is it? I haven't once sat with strangers and not heard that question in some form or other." *It's the type of question you always get asked if you hang around people too long.*

Jack cut in. "'Have you been bitten?' My pet peeve question. Topical though."

"'Have you got any food?'" Eilish said, "that's always a fun one."

"It's been such a long time since anybody asked me anything," Fin said. "The danger, I find, is not with the people themselves, rather what losing them does to you." He picked up his can of beer, confident he had enough soakage in his stomach to take a swig. "I was at work. That's the short answer. In Westport."

A man sitting on the lichen-covered stone wall of the

ringfort cleared his throat for attention. He was one of the oldest people Fin had come across in months. His brow wrinkled at rest, his skin was sallow and his hair was light as mist. "What point in time can you single out and say, 'That's it, that's when things started falling apart'?"

Jack scoffed. "When you saw somebody balling their eyes out and your first response wasn't to help, but run away."

The old man shrugged. "There were plenty of moments when you thought, 'There's no way it can get worse.' Those were almost pleasant, you acclimatised to terrible. One of the highlights for the history books – if anybody survives this to write about what happened here – is if they managed to keep the weepers from spreading outside Ireland."

"That might be it for me," Eilish said. "The moment we knew we were alone. When the world was okay with letting a nation die."

"Yes, but if it actually works and prevents this plague from spreading, I could forgive them," the old man said. "I would not wish this to be repeated anywhere else on earth. I don't know if it has spread. If so, what's the point?"

"We're not alone!" The woman that had shot down the farming idea stood up. Her colourful rain jacket crinkled as she stormed off. "We work all day and then have to listen to this doom and gloom. It's so boring." She disappeared into one of the larger tents.

Jack raised his beer at her passing. "I remember in the beginning watching as it started out slow–"

"Slow?" Eilish interrupted. "There was nothing slow about it. It spread through us like fire through a parched wood, doused in petrol. There was nothing natural about it, either. Even if you could convince me that it just popped into existence, then how do you explain the response to it?

You don't just keep something like this in one country. Not in the modern age. Oh, and it all conveniently happened during a storm, so all planes and most boats were grounded. Awfully convenient timing, no?"

Fin stopped chewing. The weight of the flash drive and all its secrets hanging from his neck was a constant burden. Now it felt like it glowed against his skin and whispered, aching to be known. "I have a good idea of how it started."

"Okay, please, no conspiracy theories," Jack said. "All I was getting at was that it happened slowly enough for us to watch as politicians regressed back to people and started looking after their own – well, more publicly than usual."

"The world didn't end with a bang," Fin said. "It must have been an infectious cough. I like to imagine it was one of those dry, scratchy, awkward ones that you can't get rid of, really makes you stand out in a crowd. Do you know the hardest question I've gotten was not what you'd expect? 'How many did you kill?' That's an easy one, I count their faces when I close my eyes, and when I dream, they get a second chance at me. Honestly, the hardest question to answer is 'What day is it?' I'm not even sure of the month anymore. For me, the world ended the last time I saw Solene. I just didn't know it at the time."

* * *

The fire crackled behind a ring of soot-blackened stones. Fin leaned forward to allow a man to pass behind him. He came back from the dark and cool trees with moss-covered firewood and fed the flames. Fin watched the sparks rise into the canopy of ancient oak and apple trees. *Will we survive to see fruit?*

"Is the heat worth the light?" Fin asked. He could not

remember the man's name. You learned quickly that memorising names was a waste of time. It was impossible to forget them.

"The dead are already watching us," Jack said. "They can't swim, so the cold is our immediate threat. The risk is worth the comfort. Hard to work when you haven't slept the previous night. Shivering costs calories. Everything must be accounted for."

"No need to scare the children with talk of them watching," the old man said.

"I'm not out to scare anybody. It's the truth. Keeping things from them might make it easier to sleep now, but they need to be prepared. They're watching. Even when they're not, treat them like they are."

Fin could sense the background tension. His first impression was that these people were good and looked out for each other, but they were people and they were all dealing with loss and regret and were facing their mortality.

"How can you possibly know that they're watching us in the dark? It's not as if their eyes glow." The man Fin suspected had arrived not long before him spoke for the first time.

"How did you survive this long? Assume they're always listening, always watching," Jack said.

"Paranoia is no way to live."

Jack threw his arms up in exasperation. "It's the only way to live, you absolute gobshite. Don't you worry though, stick around. I'm paranoid enough for all of us."

Fin felt that same paranoia on the river. The small hairs on his body nearly continuously at attention. It was exhausting, always checking over your shoulder, jumping at every noise. Instinct was a body language that he was only just learning to understand. "Have any of you encountered... intelligent infected?"

Eerie silence was his answer. He imagined the shivers were a shared sensation around the fire.

"How do you mean, intelligent?" Jack asked.

It was only a feeling, and not one that Fin was willing to have his mental health questioned over. "I've had a few strange encounters that would make you wonder what's going on in their heads."

"If I hadn't just gone for a piss, I'd need new underwear," someone said. "The way you were going on, I thought you were about to tell us that you saw weepers hiding in bushes, holding string attached to a box on a stick, hovering over a crate of beer."

"Jack would have died in the first week if that were the case," Eilish said. "It wouldn't be a bad idea to treat the weepers like they've just been awarded college degrees. Whatever keeps you alive."

Too often Fin had dissuaded himself from the idea that they retained some level of intelligence, only to swear he spotted a familiar one. "I'm pretty sure that some of them have been tracking me down the river."

"Ah now you're talking ghost stories, not a bad one mind," Jack said. "If the weepers had any sense at all, then we'd all be wandering the country slack-jawed like them."

Fin remained silent; he did not have to convince them. He was barely able to believe it himself. "So the fact that weepers and zombies exist doesn't faze you, but the possibility that some of them didn't lose all their marbles is completely beyond belief?"

Before Jack could respond, Eilish did. "You could buy the exact same jacket in every town and city across the country in identical clothing chains. That could've been what you saw."

"Maybe," Fin allowed. He cheered up momentarily as he tried to believe it.

Around the ringfort there was a mix of shoddily constructed rafts made from empty barrels and wooden pallets. Deflated boats and pool toys were flattened out to dry. There was a small one-person sailing craft hauled onto the land. Fin could see the mast through the trees. Only one vessel had an onboard engine, but the noise would draw so many weepers that it would strand them on the lake for days.

The ringfort acted as a windbreaker. The branches overhead shivered in the breeze, the gentle rustling sounded too similar to the stalking dead. In the dark there was little difference between a settled zombie and an exhausted survivor. Though they were hardly harmless. *There are no innocent survivors.* It was a harsh way of looking at people, but it kept him alive. He leaned back against his battered kayak. When he closed his eyes for too long his heart rate rose until they snapped open. He desperately needed sleep, but he doubted he would find any.

The people here could not endure silence for long. The relaxing banter was a small bit of civilisation Fin had gone without for too long. Despite his hesitation towards others, he felt a kinship with them.

The light cast haunting shadows through the trees. The ghosts of old had no grip on him, not now, after being steeped in terror for so long. The sound of lake water lapping over warbling stones calmed him. *The dead don't swim.* Fin listened to the noise of the natural world, but as soothing as that was, he could not sit idle. He needed to know what lay ahead, he needed their stories. They too would want to hear about what awaited them. He felt that anybody tracing back his steps would surely die. It was with grim realisation that he was certain they felt the same of him heading east.

The whiskey finally made its way around the fire and back to him. It was considerably lighter. The bottle was cold to the touch, but it would keep them warm for the night. He poured himself a shot. Then took out another bottle from his kayak. An expensive, top-shelf brand, not that that mattered now.

"Survival essentials," Eilish said when she saw the size of the second bottle.

"You might joke, but a hangover has saved my life more times than I'm comfortable with." *And been the death of more than I can bear.* The thought stole his brief smile. There was a measurable drop in dread as the drink loosened them. If they were like Fin then they would soon stop worrying about what they had survived and become thankful that they had survived. But it was only putting dread off until morning.

He took a blackened pot from his kayak and excused himself. Walking towards the shore was slow work, the fire had robbed him of his night eyes. All heat had left him before he reached the water. *This is dangerous, lad. You want to get back to the fire. Soon you'll want to stay with them. Why not, sure?*

He knelt and filled the pot. Somewhere in the darkness a bird took flight. It danced across the surface of the lake. Its wings cut the air with a velveteen rasp as it flew overhead. Fin could not make out anything that might have disturbed it, but he did not start breathing normally again until he was back in the camp. He placed the pot to boil.

"What did all of you do before this?" Fin asked. "I was a

night porter." He took a small sip of the whiskey. It stung his cracked lips and scalded the back of his throat. "Though if we're going for complete honesty, I was a terrible one."

Sap inside one of the logs erupted with a crack and a small constellation of sparks rose into the night, before the cold extinguished them. Somebody poked the dead wood until it crumpled into the bed of glowing embers.

"Beautiful sky out tonight," Eilish said. She got comfortable once her cup was full of whiskey and lay in a bed of crinkled leaves.

Fin looked up through the clearing of trees. The bulbous moon hung overhead, eavesdropping on their conversation. It was so clear he could map every imperfection scarred across its surface. "If you were really stretched to look for a positive in all this, the night sky is astonishing these days," he said.

"The whole country is a dark sky reserve. Amateur astronomers are trying to hide their delight," Eilish said. "The ones that are still alive. I was an overnight garage attendant. Worked in the arse end of nowhere."

"Those trucks in town, are they yours?" Fin asked.

"No. The roads are completely impassable. Only things worth a damn on wheels now are bikes and scooters."

"I'm desperate to find a pair of those shoes with wheels in the heels," Jack said, generating a laugh from the others.

Without a word, Ian came out of the shadows to pour some whiskey into a flask and then walked back from the light.

When the water in the battered pot boiled, Fin took out his hot water bottle and carefully filled it. After he tucked it beneath his jumper he noticed all eyes on him. "What?"

"That's a million dollar idea," Jack said.

"It has been the difference between life and death a few times," Fin said.

"I was a student," one man spoke up just as the whiskey bottle reached him. His unibrow was slowly starting to fill in. His ragged stubble was turning into a scraggly beard of red and brown. He was hesitant to pass the bottle when a young teenager went to take it. Her parents were not present to deny her and to try to fill that role had the potential to cause more harm than a cup full of whiskey could.

Some in the group laughed when she spluttered after she drank. The atmosphere seemed more normal by the minute. Fin found no humour in it. He stood up, crossed the ring and took the cup from her. Exchanging it for an unopened bottle of soda. "Don't let your guard down. Don't dull your senses or fuddle your inhibitions. You'd be wrong to think all the rapists are dead." There were no accusations at his outburst. "Cut your hair, too."

"I don't want to cut my hair. I wear hats so the weepers can't grab it," she said.

Fin walked back to his kayak, cheeks burning from the attention. He sat down with a grunt, old bruises twinged, his hip ached from a fall that had not healed properly. "Say they knock your hat off and you're bald, then you have a chance to get away. Sometimes all we can hope for is a bit of luck."

Eilish spoke up. "We make our own luck. Don't wait for it. Look at me, I won the lottery." She waved a tattered and worn ticket in the air.

"I don't know that I'd call winning the lottery just as the world ended good luck," Fin said.

"Hang on, they never got to call the last draw. It was supposed to be the day after storm Peggy," Jack said.

She winked at him. "I promise you, this is my winning ticket. My luck."

The bottle finally made its way back to Fin. He could already feel it loosening his nerves. Somewhere in the distance they heard the desperate weeping of an infected. Sound travelled far in a dying land. Silence took on a unique aspect when it was almost all-encompassing.

Fin topped up his cup and sent the whiskey around the ring again. "I'd like to hear that story."

Warm food, a fire and alcohol put all of them in a mood for stories. Those in their tents, wrapped in blankets and rustling sleeping bags, stopped their private conversations to listen.

More weepers took up the call of the hunt on the mainland. It had a withering effect on those that heard it. Fin raised his can of beer as a toast, hoping that the monsters had only found a fox or badger.

"I wonder what this ringfort meant to the people that built it," Jack said to drown out the weeping. "It's quite amazing."

"My granddad used to tell me that they were pathways to other worlds," Fin said.

"I wish," Eilish smiled. "Travel across rivers was probably the best option hundreds of years ago, when the country was covered with trees. They could have been way stations."

"Stop stalling. You're after telling us that we're sitting with a millionaire. Let's hear the story," Jack said.

"It started with a storm called Peggy."

3

LUCKY TICKET

"How warm was it today, do you remember?" Phyllis asked.

"Oh, I don't know. It was cold, if that helps," Eilish said.

"Pick two numbers for me."

"Seven and eight."

"Oh, put a bit more thought into it, please. This could be our winning ticket."

Eilish tried to hide her amusement at how flustered Phyllis became if she suspected you did not invoke some form of divination to choose numbers randomly. She scanned the woman's groceries and read out the numbers.

Phyllis rubbed the foil off some scratch cards, leaving a dusting of dark flakes on the counter. Eilish wished that anything could excite in her the same joy that Phyllis got from those cards. It turned out to be a dud. "Ah, better luck next time," Phyllis said.

"Maybe." Each week Eilish watched her gamble more of her pension on those tickets than she ever did on food or fuel. *What good is a couple of million to you anyway? You'd just buy more tickets.* Eilish bagged the shopping and carried it out to the car. A strong wind caught the door and strained its hinges. Now-defunct newspapers were ruffled by the gust.

"That weather would take your life," Phyllis said. She turned her hood up and hunched over more than she usually did.

"Going out in this hardly seems worth the risk for some chocolate digestives and tea bags!" Eilish had to shout to be heard above the storm.

Phyllis laughed. "And the lottery," she winked. "Weather like this, half the usual players probably won't be bothered with it. I'm guaranteed to win."

Is there ever a time you don't think you've got the winning ticket? "Well remember me when you've made your millions." She did not have the heart to tell her that most people had the sense to play online.

Phyllis's small car was older than Eilish. She put the bags in the boot and braced the driver's door open for her. Old air fresheners were a pungent presence that weighed down the rear-view mirror. "Be careful getting home." The rain beyond the petrol pump shelter fell in thick sheets of fat, needle-sharp and frigid droplets. The ditches would soon fill and spill out, covering winding country roads, blinding the cat's eyes and covering the road markings.

As soon as she drove off, the red tail-lights were swallowed by the storm. Without the shopping bags to balance her, Eilish had to stand at an angle to keep on her feet. Trees in the adjacent fields swayed and creaked. She expected her apartment would be without electricity for the holiday. *More incentive to be working.* She locked the gas cylinder cage and closed the coal and turf bins. The light of the petrol station was the only beacon in the night.

There was little time before her guests arrived. She hurried about her duties; the newspapers were baled, keeping one out for herself. She only ever skimmed the paper to see that things were still happening in the world, though she usually experienced a horrible feeling of missing out.

After she restocked the shelves, swept and mopped the floor, that was essentially her work done for the shift. With the storm worsening, she expected a quiet night. Eilish went to the back office to wrap presents. Finding Christmas paper with little trucks and lorries on it was nearly better than what they would cover. Once finished, she set them under a small plastic Christmas tree on the deli counter.

The first visitor arrived on time. Martin gave his cheerful knock. It was difficult to miss him in his high-visibility vest. "It's bitter out there. Holy fuck. That storm will be the death of me," Martin said.

"How are the roads?"

"Brutal. Sure any grit they put down in case of ice is probably blown halfway across the Irish Sea. The truck has a new braking system. As soon as wind pushes you one way, the brakes come on on the other side to compensate. I must have drifted most of the way from Dublin. How has work been?"

"Dead. The only people coming out are those that ran out of pet food or need to get their scratch card fix. Coffee?" Eilish asked.

"You mean that ditch water you make? Yes, go on."

While the pale, overly milky cappuccino squirted from the gurgling machine, the lights of a massive lorry shone through the ink thick darkness. Derek greeted them by flashing his high beams, flooding the store with stunning light.

"He's an awful bastard," Martin said.

Derek parked his lorry around back. The station was a

waypoint for lonely truckers and long haulers. They were the invisible elves that ensured that shelves in stores nationwide were full. Eilish envied their commutes; travelling the country, ghosting through villages, towns and cities. Unseen, but for others in the trade, night shift workers, badgers, bats, owls and foxes.

"Merry Christmas." Derek was a heavyset man, with terrible arm tattoos, which he swore he did not do himself. Most of them were the Liverpool football team crest and slogans. He had the birthdays of his children and an ex's name poorly covered by a new woman's face. Though Eilish wondered how fond he could really be of her if he displayed that depiction openly. The man never seemed to have a bad day, his shell-shocked, bright, blue eyes seemed constantly effervescent with cheer.

"Merry Christmas. How's the family?" Eilish asked.

"Which one?" He laughed every time he made that joke. "Ah, they're all good. School's going well and Sasha has her first loose tooth. That's why I took a few extra shifts, she keeps coming up to me and wobbling it with her tongue. She won't be laughing when I get sick on her."

"She'll remember that when you start losing your teeth," Martin said.

"Nah, she'll be too busy worrying about changing my nappy at that stage."

"Not long off." Martin offered him the paper that he had been flicking through.

Derek sighed. "Don't I know it."

"Coffee?" She already had the cup at the ready.

"You mean that warmed-up water you drained from a bag of coal left outside all winter?"

Eilish smiled. "You complain about it, but remember

that one time the machine wasn't working and you swore never to come back here again?"

"The tongue would be hanging out of your head with thirst if you waited for the next station," Derek said.

"You have other petrol station hostesses?"

"You took the news better than my wife did when she discovered I'd other families."

"She was probably delighted there was somebody else with firsthand experience of your shite. They probably started a support group."

Derek washed up behind the deli counter and started making sandwiches. Before he finished, a van pulled into the station, shortly followed by a truck. "I'm convinced they hide down the road, waiting until lunch is made for them," Derek said.

Grace and Matthew came in together. Matthew buried his hands beneath his armpits. "It's rough," he said in a thick North Dublin accent. He was tall and skinny, with a head of blond stubble. His new earring had cost him an earful of abuse from the group, but it would only get worse if he took it out because of them. A little older than Eilish, he was new to the vans.

Grace locked the door behind her. Her long, brown, curly hair came out in a messy nest when she took her old holey hat off. She made straight for the heater and leaned against it. "I'm going to settle down here for the night, I suggest the rest of you do too. It's too dangerous out there. Passed a few Garda cars blaring lights in front of downed trees. I don't think there's enough hazard signs in Ireland for every tree that will fall tonight. Wouldn't want to be working with the electrical company. They'll be earning their money."

"I don't know," Matthew said. "My supervisor kept

hinting that no storm would keep him from making deliveries."

"A lad in the head office is it?" Martin asked. "Don't listen to a word they say. Right now he's tucked up in his warm bed. His missus will be left wanting after he's spent from fucking you over. Tell them the roads are blocked. Wouldn't be a lie."

"They check the GPS on my van. They'll ask why I didn't try another route." Matthew sounded like his arm had been sufficiently twisted already.

"Well if they try to sack you for not driving in dangerous conditions, you'd have a tidy sum when you sue them. Just remind them of that," Derek said.

"And not subtly," Grace added. "Half of those pricks only understand numbers. The closest the other half have ever gotten to a truck is the model on their desks."

A speed camera van pulled into the garage. "Quick put the lights out," Derek said as the driver came in. "Ah Frank, you bastard. How are things? How many people had their days ruined by you so far?"

"I'd love to say that it was a slow day at the office," he smiled. It got a chuckle from Derek, which he tried to stifle. "I've never seen so many people speed past the camera. Most of them didn't even bother slowing down when they saw me. Despite plenty of Good Samaritans flashing their lights to warn them. Nearly flashed the lights on the speed van myself."

"Are you serious?" Eilish asked.

Frank rocked on his feet. "It's the strangest thing. Normally you'd see people burning rubber, putting the brakes on when they see me. At one point I wondered if there was a race on and I'd been sent to the track as a joke."

"Last minute shoppers," Grace said. "The fear that

comes from leaving the presents until the very last minute does terrible things to a person."

"There are a rake of naughty letters on their way out now," Frank said.

"I know people should generally take pride in their work. But you probably shouldn't openly express yours," Derek said.

"Come here to me, I didn't force anybody to speed. You'd swear in your head I do be waving a black and white checkered flag beside the van, goading people to go faster."

Eilish interrupted them. In the past, their playful volley had occasionally turned into proper arguments. Derek was still sore about past speeding tickets and treated all speed camera operators with disdain. "I've a present for you all," Eilish said. She brought a large box out of the office. "A brand new coffee machine just for us. You lot are always giving out about the muck we serve, so I thought I'd treat you all to a nice cup when you arrive."

Derek laughed. "What are we supposed to give out about now?"

"I'm sure you'll think of something." Eilish plugged it in and gave each of them their small present from under the tree. The truck wrapping paper was appreciated. Derek guffawed when he saw Frank's race car mug. Each of them got a mug with a picture of their vehicle type on it.

"You shouldn't have," Grace said.

Eilish waved her off. "It's not much."

"Frank, I got you a little something too," Derek said.

"Here we go."

Derek took out a roll of flame decals. "For the side of your speed van."

Grace laughed and gave Frank a small package. Inside was a large red button with the word NITROUS written on it. "Doesn't actually do anything, but it makes those fast noises we know you love."

"Lads, I'm not a speed freak." Frank grinned.

Matthew awkwardly held out a small envelope to Frank. Eilish thought it was a Christmas card until she heard Frank's excitement. "You didn't have to go to this much bother."

They crowded around to get a look at the card. It was a coupon for a couple of laps around a race track.

"That's a present for the lot of us," Derek said. "You finally get to let off a bit of steam over the speed limit."

"I got one for all of you," Matthew said. "Got them on special offer."

Eilish prepared fancy coffees in their new mugs while presents were exchanged. When she finished, they all stood looking at her. Grace held out a package.

Eilish bit her tongue. "Let me guess, an air freshener and a small model truck?"

They smiled, but gave nothing away. The package was heavy. She tore open the paper, conscious of her cheeks burning from their attention. It was a college textbook. Year one. All humour left as the sincerity of the gift hit her. "Thank you so much."

"Open it," Grace said.

The thought that she had to commit most of the heavy book to memory was mildly daunting, considering it was only for one module. There was a message on the front cover.

Dear Eilish,
May this drive you just a little further along the
route to your dreams. The same way that

muck you call coffee does for us on a cold night.
All our love.

In place of signatures there were badly drawn pictures of a speed camera van, two lorries. a delivery truck and a post van.

There was an envelope from each of them inside. Speechless, she opened them. There was a cheque in all but one, the last envelope was a voucher for a spin on a race track from Matthew. The combined amount was the equivalent of three months' savings for her.

"Eh, don't shake mine," Matthew said awkwardly. "It's a ticket to the racecourse. They were on special offer."

"Don't sell yourself short, you got the book," Derek said. "Damn things are so expensive. You'd swear they were printed on gold leaf."

"I can't accept this. It's way too much."

"Oh, okay then," Derek made to take the book back, but closed the cover instead. "We're sick of hearing you moan about the pay here. Be a nice change to start hearing you complain about the cost of living in Dublin."

Grace elbowed him in the side. "No point putting it off any longer. Go in, do your time and come out into something you're interested in. Better still, get out of Ireland."

Eilish hugged them all in turn and tried to wipe away tears before they formed. "You're a pack of bastards. I knew we should have set a spending limit. You know I got that coffee machine in the sales." Before she hugged Frank, she asked, "When you keep mentioning your other family, you're not hinting that I'm your…"

"Feck off. So does this mean we get the fresh food? Not the shite that has been mouldering in the open for the day?" Derek asked.

* * *

The night passed quickly, with everybody sheltering out of the storm there. They set up for a game of cards after dinner. If they played for actual money, Eilish would have lost more than they had given her for college. The storm became savage. Rain fell in an impenetrable veil that sounded like it could erode the world. They could barely make out the lights of the pumps through the warped windows.

Eilish lit candles and took out a few batteries for her torch in preparation for the inevitable. The wax had barely started to trickle down the side of the candles when the power failed.

Derek rifled through his pockets for his phone. "That's odd. There's a push notification on my screen warning about a new flu. Did any of you get the same?" Without the hum of the refrigerators, they could hear the wrath of the wind.

They all had the same warning. "Perfect timing," Grace said. "Just when the holidays start. I bet you anything I'll catch it the moment I finish up."

"Wonder how much taxpayers' money went towards warning people about a bout of the snuffles," Derek said.

Nobody wanted to get him started on the government, so Grace changed the topic. "What happens now with the power out?"

"There's a generator out the back to keep the freezers working. The petrol pumps are dead though until power returns. Not that anybody would be out in this." She lit a few more candles and placed them on the counter. "Are we still playing?"

There was light on the road. A car sped past so quickly that Eilish thought it must be a Garda patrol car. Not even boy racers risked the bendy roads here.

"What the hell was he playing at?" Derek said. "I know I take the mickey out of you, Frank, but I wish you had your camera on to catch that fool."

The soothing wash of candlelight and calming sound of the storm made Eilish yawn. Before they could play another hand of cards, a car pulled into the garage. The driver never dipped his high beams, blinding them. The car skidded to a halt in front of a petrol pump. The driver got out without closing his door and ran around to fill his tank. When the pump did not work, he started behaving erratically.

Derek was up in an instant and banged on the glass. "Oi mate! What are you at?"

The man jumped at the noise, his legs nearly buckled. He ran towards them and tried the locked door. "Let me in!"

"There's not a hope of you coming in here in that state. Calm down," Derek said.

The man surprised them all when he started crying. He hammered on the door, kicked and begged.

"Cop on. Throwing a tantrum isn't going to help. Back away or I'll call the Gardaí."

"You've killed us. I'm nearly out of fuel." The man hurried back to his car and came back wielding a large kitchen knife. "Let me in!"

Chairs squealed across the tiles as everybody stood up. "Eilish, call the cops," Derek said. He stepped away from the door, shocked by the man's fury.

Eilish turned the flashlight on and shone it directly in

his face. She recognised him. "Mitchell? The power's out. The pumps won't work. We can't help you."

He flinched from the sound or mention of his name.

"Please – I'm begging you. I need fuel." He spun around, startled by something. He put his hand up for them to be quiet. It was only then that Eilish noticed the woman and child in the car. She was screaming at him to get back in. All colour bled from his face. "Damn you." He hurried back to the car and sped off into the night, leaving the front of the garage in darkness.

Grace was upset. "Does that often happen when you're on your own?"

"That was a first."

"We have to report him, did you see the woman and child in the car?" Frank said. He took out his phone to make a call but dropped it when Matthew yelled.

"Somebody's watching us."

4

SURVIVORS

"Hang on. I thought you were in the midlands," Jack said. "How did the infection get down to you so fast?"

Still lying on her back, Eilish put her hand up to blot out the moon, pressing the stars one by one with her fingertips. She took a moment to compose herself. Nobody rushed her. "You're not one of those people that believes the storm caused the weepers?" She turned over onto her elbows to inquire after Jack's silence. "You're not?"

"I operated cranes for a living, I don't have any opinion on what started this. You'd want a doctor, scientist or – more likely – a priest for that."

Eilish lay back down. "The first incident wasn't in Dublin either. I heard it was a village in Cork, but that's just a rumour. I met somebody recently who thought it started in their neighbour's house in County Laois."

"Can we not speculate over how it began?" Jack asked. "I've spent countless nights with different groups, wasting time, wondering about that."

"Storm Peggy didn't start the epidemic, but it kept it from

becoming a pandemic," Eilish said. "Flights were grounded and no boats left port. Not in those swells. I suppose I wouldn't blame somebody for thinking it was biblical. The response just seemed so quick. Aid rushed in not long after the news broke. And how do you explain all the warships getting here so fast? They send aid in and we stay put. There's plenty of blame, we just need to find the neck to hang the noose on."

"How's that aid treating you?" Fin asked. The spite in his tone surprised him.

"I know we're all already firm friends," Jack said. "But, I'd hoped it would have at least taken us a day to start squabbling about this."

Fin yawned and pulled the zip of his jacket up a little higher beneath his chin. He was no closer to sleep than he had been on the river. Some of those sitting around the fire struggled to keep their heads from nodding. He watched them with envy.

"You came from Westport?" a woman asked. Her voice was quiet, barely interrupting the silence around the fire. "I heard there was a camp there. Are people safe?"

Fin stared back at the ring of eyes. The full moon overhead glared, unable to blink or turn away from the horrors it passed across the doom of Ireland. *What's it like in the rest of the world? Do they think of us now without the news crews to show them the privation of a nation of dispossessed peasants? How many people are looking up at that same moon now from ditches? Locked away in houses they do not own. Destitute and starving. Too hungry for the moon's beauty to hold any sway over them. Too bright. Light to die by.*

"There was a camp. Despite their precautions – it fell. I reckon you won't see many more uninfected coming from that way. The dead hold the west. This is the first camp I've encountered in a long time. As nice as it is here, if I didn't have to rest, I wouldn't stop."

The woman bowed her head and said nothing. *I could have been gentler with that.* He squeezed his hands together and desperately tried to banish the memories of the fallen camp. *If anything, I put it too gently. Whoever she's thinking about is probably already gone. Who am I to talk? My people are likely dead. Hope is all that's keeping us going.* "Obviously, I'm not the only one to escape. Worry about finding others after this ends. Anybody with an ounce of sense would head down to Kerry. Mountain valleys, low population."

"Nothing to eat," Eilish added.

Fin nodded at that. "Seems like the only ones with full bellies these days are the weepers."

"Why are you going east then?" Eilish asked. "The most densely populated region and you're heading straight for it."

"I never said I had any sense." Fin fished in his kayak for another bottle of whiskey. He handed it around, confident that there was not enough in the bottles to get the group more than just a little tipsy. The effects would wear off by morning.

Ian ruined the mood by rushing into the clearing. From his whispered tone and the way he carried himself, they knew there was trouble. "Movement on the shore," he said.

"Weeper or human?" Fin asked. He threw out what remained in his cup.

"Both. But the survivors are making that much noise that there'll only be weepers soon."

"What do we do?" Eilish asked.

The brief silence was reassuring in a way. *There is no surviving without guilt.* "A few weeks ago, I would have said whatever we can," Fin said.

Now that they were listening out for it, the people on the

shore were so loud that they could hear them speaking from the heart of the island. The group formed a solemn line and followed Ian to the water's edge. It took a few seconds for the ghost of the fire to leave Fin's vision.

"They're going to get themselves killed," Eilish said. "I'm of a mind that stupidity can't be allowed to catch on."

The sound of panic made the group bow their heads. They could stay silent in the warmth and relative safety of their island, but Fin wondered how poisonous guilt could really be. Given enough time, he knew it could be lethal.

"I'll use a rowboat and head over," Fin said. "No engines. They might start shouting if they hear one. Who will come with me? We won't go too near the shore. They can swim to us."

Ian nodded and Eilish stepped forward.

"What if –" Jack began.

"I'll stop you there," Fin said. "If we start going into the what ifs, we'll be here until sunrise."

"I was going to say, 'What if I head out on my paddleboard and lure the infected away?'"

"Appreciate it." Fin helped Ian drag a boat to the shore. Without the fire, he quickly felt the night deep in his body. *Too much of that is as demoralising as hunger.* Ian passed life jackets to Fin, Jack and Eilish. Jack left first. Eilish got into the boat as Fin and Ian pushed it out before jumping in. Water spilled over the rim of Fin's boots and drenched his socks. He was constantly searching for clean ones.

"What do we do if these aren't pleasant people?" Eilish asked.

Fin took a small knife from his belt and revealed the pistol he had taken out of the kayak with the second bottle of whiskey and hidden in his jacket.

"That will probably make them friendly," Eilish said.

She seemed wary of him now. "Are you much of a shot with it?"

Fin smiled to try and put her at ease. "It's not really the best tool to practice with these days. Hammer and knife are better for dealing with weepers. If you use a gun, you may as well use it on yourself for the amount of trouble you'll bring." He was conscious that these people were still strangers. He had known desperate people – briefly. Had seen firsthand what despair could do to a person. He gritted his teeth. "You don't have to be much of a shot at close range."

The message was clear and received with silence. Fin and Eilish each took an oar. Ian watched the shore to find the survivors.

They rowed in tandem, making corrections at Ian's suggestion. There were two survivors. Both men. They had climbed over fences that partitioned fields. Those would slow the zombies, but would not hold the weepers back for long.

There was movement beneath the trees all along the shore. The survivors were being hunted. There was no more time for subtlety. Ian turned his torch on and off in quick bursts.

"Somebody's out there. Hey, over here! Help!"

Ian turned to face those in the boat and shook his head. "We may turn around. Those fools are going to get all of us killed. Quiet!" He spoke as loudly as he dared, but they were too overwhelmed with relief to listen.

"Hurry up! They're following us."

The sound of breathless weeping echoed from the treeline. No matter how often Fin heard it, it still made his skin ripple with goosebumps. Before the outbreak he would have thought it was a vixen wailing, or the tender keening of somebody completely bereaved. The only other sound came from water lapping against the side of the boat.

The survivors churned the water in the shallows as they waded out into the freezing lake. Fast silhouettes rushed out towards the shore. Disorientated, some ran away from them. One stopped and listened. "Not intelligent, my ass," Fin said. He swallowed bile.

The weeper followed the noise and picked up speed when it saw the men trying to escape. Its pace and inhuman, shambling gait was horrible to witness. Weepers did not have the restrictions that self-preservation put on a body. It stumbled and fell in its haste, too keen to kill to concentrate on its footing.

Most of the other weepers followed her. It tumbled head first over the wire mesh fence, entering the field with the survivors.

"Bring the boat closer!" one of them screamed.

"I don't want to die," the other said, repeating it over and over, as if saying it would make it so.

"Swim," Fin said. "We're not bringing the boat in. This is as much risk as we're taking."

The closest weeper got back to its feet. It was winded and no longer able to weep. Fin took shorter, shallow breaths and made sure his mask was on properly. There had been no studies done of the weepers. If they were in other countries, the results had never made it to Ireland.

A cacophony of weeping echoed throughout the woods. It was impossible to tell how many there were. More came out from beneath the trees and ran straight into the water. Fin assumed they were disoriented by the moonlight after being under a muffling spring canopy.

The crisp sound of a ringing bell cracked through the echoing cold. Jack managed to lure some of the infected away. Though there were too many of them, they were frenzied and focused on the survivors.

The weepers did not flinch when they entered the lake, but the water made them unsteady. Those that fell stopped weeping, unable to pick themselves up.

"Swim or die," Ian said.

With no other options, they committed themselves to the lake. One man threw his hammer towards the weepers before diving in, he gasped and shivered when he surfaced. The hammer landed harmlessly in the grass.

When they reached the boat, they tried frantically to climb aboard. Eilish was the first to greet them with her knife. She buried the tip into the wood between their hands. "Empty your pockets."

Both men shook violently, their breath frosted in the moonlight. The sound of the weepers made them compliant. "It's freezing, help us in. I can't feel my fingers."

"You won't have any fingers if you don't empty your fucking pockets," Eilish said.

The man glared at her, but reached into his pocket and pulled out a knife. His fingers trembled. He dropped it into the boat. Eilish said nothing, she just stared at him expectantly.

The other man pressed his forehead against the wood of the boat. "I don't want to die."

"Did you not hear her?" Ian asked.

The man nodded and threw in a pair of scissors and two knives. "I don't have anything else. He has a filleting knife down his trouser leg. Another taped to his back and one up his left sleeve."

The other man stared at his friend in disbelief. There was no point in denying it. The weapons were quickly handed over. Fin was becoming accustomed to liars. There was no telling if they had planned this as an emergency tactic. Perhaps they had further weapons hidden and told them about these ones to gain trust. Either way the cold was sapping their resolve.

"Please help us."

"Lad, do you not think the weepers have made us numb to sympathy?" Ian asked. "Their cries pull at the heart strings more than your bitching does. Be quiet."

The three of them pulled the survivors in one at a time, checking each for concealed weapons. They made the survivors row. Despite what Ian said, Fin did feel for them. The dark robbed their faces of detail. These two survived weepers, to be picked up by people who, from appearances, seemed completely indifferent to their plight. They had no food or supplies on them to barter. *They'll lie about having a store of it somewhere. They're just mouths to feed.*

"Put these on." Fin threw them scraps of ragged cloth to cover their mouths. "How many of you are there?" He saw Ian stare at him from behind them.

They hunched up from the cold, shivering as they rowed to the island. Part of having them working the oars was to ensure they could not get up to mischief. The other part was to keep their blood flowing until they could get close to the fire.

"There's only two of us now. We ran out of food." The man's teeth chattered so much that they clicked together when he spoke.

They got little from the other man, who set about rowing so vigorously away from the shore that the boat started turning away from the island. It made sense to Fin that these two were not long out of hiding. Those that survived knew to be silent. *These two might just have won the lottery by running into this group.*

*　*　*

Ian jumped out of the boat and dragged it onto the shore. The men followed, trying to show that they could be useful. Their shoes squelched when they moved. Eilish brought them straight through to the camp. They slowed when they met the others with their weapons ready. When nothing was said, they dropped down close to the fire. Before anybody could ask them to strip, one of the survivors covered his face in his hands and started crying. The other closed his eyes and savoured the heat.

People left them to their grief and went through their meagre possessions to find spare dry clothing. Two plastic cups were filled with whiskey and cans of beer were left beside them. The crying man looked up pitifully at the person handing him the beer and said, "I don't want to die."

"Welcome to the club, mate. There's fresh clothes laid out in the tent over there. Why don't you get changed? You'll warm up a lot faster."

The man nodded, downed the whiskey, took the beer and went to the tent. The other man stayed by the fire. He stole glances towards the tent. Fin wondered if he was still sore about having to give away his secret weapons.

The little acts of kindness were enough to bolster the mood of the group. When offered food, the man nearly choked in his haste to eat it. Fin felt nauseated watching him, knowing how cruel he must have appeared on the water. *What does it matter? They're alive.*

"Slow down there," somebody said. "You'll only do yourself harm if you've not eaten for a while."

"That's nonsense," Ian said. "How can you harm somebody dying of hunger by giving them food?"

"Just something I vaguely remember from a documentary, or might have been a film. Not sure if it's true. Overfeeding somebody that is starving could hurt them."

"I think you're right," somebody else said. "I remember hearing a story about concentration camps, when they were liberated, the soldiers couldn't give the prisoners too much food."

The survivor stopped eating at the mention of prisoners.

Ian sat down hard. He wiped his hand down his face and pulled the dirty old mask off to let cool air in. He licked his lips and stretched his mouth to ward off tears. "You're sure?"

The man nodded. Ian continued.

"I nearly killed somebody the other day. She was shuffling around like a zombie. She had that distant stare that sees nothing. When she noticed me, she reached out. She had less vigour than a weeper and just about more balance than a zombie. I managed to turn the swing of my hammer away from her head after I copped that her fingers were bloodless. She was starving. Her clothes probably weighed more than she did."

"What did you do?" Eilish asked.

"I gave her what I had, I was strong enough to find more. Maybe it was just in my head, but it looked like she was hoping to find weepers."

"You can't be soft. Giving her your food like that. There's enough around here to feed all of us, why did she not look?" Eilish asked.

Ian shook his head. "Leave off. You didn't see those eyes. If she survives, she'll never be the same. None of us are the people we were before this. Who hasn't known loss? Weepers don't have to bite you to kill you. Fear will do that slowly."

Fin knew he was getting further from his old self the closer he came to reaching Solene. *Will she suffer the man I'm becoming?* She was no longer just his girlfriend, he had built her up as a totem, a mantra. In times when hope was just a bitter memory, he thought of her. *Do it for Solene. The memory of you has saved me more times than I can count.* Without her, he would have simply stopped.

"Why'd you leave her out there?" Jack asked. "We could look after her."

"Have you ever seen a starving, feral cat?" Ian asked. "They'll fight tooth and nail, operating off spite alone. She was like that. Half-crazed, but desperate enough to approach me. I lured a pack of infected off the farm. Just as I'd put enough distance between me and them to not feel their breath on my neck, I found her. A few riled-up zombies I could handle, but I wasn't expecting the weepers. These ones were fast and agile. Didn't make a sound until I was nearly amongst them. I only spotted them by chance."

Fin sat up. "What do you mean?"

"You weren't here for it," Eilish said. "Our friend here is convinced that there are intelligent weepers."

Ian stared at Fin, looking for something in his face. "I wouldn't be surprised after meeting that pack. I never heard a peep out of them, the woods were mostly quiet. I genuinely thought I'd gotten rid of most of them. When they started weeping – sounded like others picked up the cry from horizon to horizon. I panicked. I set her up in a house and secured it as best I could. Left her with food, water, vitamins. Lads, I wouldn't leave until I saw her take a few vitamins. Got all the blankets in the house. Set her up well. I promise you. Couldn't leave the weepers around to gather a crowd. If both of us stayed, we would've been trapped and starved out. I wasn't sure how sane she was, what if she killed me in the night? Or brought weepers down on us?"

"Did she speak?" Jack asked.

"Not a word. She was like a ghost. I ran. I was sure I brought most of them with me. I lured them to the quarry and spent the night feeding the fish."

"Feeding the fish?" Fin said.

"There's a crane facing out over a local quarry. Nothing special, but the infected can't climb. Once you get comfy and start ringing a bell, they barely look down as they go over the edge. I spent the night there, watching them. Never made a sound except when they hit the water. I thought it would be therapeutic, watching them fall, but I can't shake the pity I feel for them. Haven't been able to get back to her yet."

Fin wondered if this was the reason he was wandering the island perimeter: hoping to spot her on the shore.

"How much food did you give her?" Jack asked.

"Everything. I kept half a bottle of water."

"How far gone was she?"

"Skin and bone, except for her belly. Don't know if she was pregnant. Could have been swollen from hunger."

Jack cursed. "When the horde clears, we'll go find her."

Ian nodded his thanks. "So giving food to somebody dying of hunger will kill them. Can't even be kind in this world."

"Focus on other things," Eilish said. "We need more food. If we could bring enough out here, we wouldn't have to leave the island. Imagine that. Build up the defences so no zombies could wash up. Start building shelters to get out of tents and off the ground."

"The infection spread so quickly that there are still houses out there with food," Fin said. "Warehouses full of the stuff for the Christmas rush. Just waiting to spoil."

Eilish shook her head. "If you look at a map of this area,

it's a beautiful tapestry of green. We aren't going to find many warehouses full of food. Too rural, too low a population density and too much empty space between towns."

"I don't know that I'd call it empty," Jack said. "You have weepers, zombies, wild animals that are possibly infected. The bastarding cold. Many nights it pitted me against the infected, just for the sake of moving to keep warm. Oh, did I forget to mention that the plants are starting to grow again? In a few more weeks fields will become grassland. In a few years the countryside will be a forest again. A squirrel will be able to make it from one end of Ireland to another without leaving the trees."

"I'm not confident about the food situation," Ian said. "The country is mostly – well, country. The infection will have taken longer to reach rural areas. Those people eat the food and have no means to resupply. Hunger sends them out in search of more. We found a few sheds of seed potatoes, even that is only a fleeting answer to our problems. When the weepers have nothing left to hunt in the towns and cities, they'll come this way."

"The way the weepers spread out takes away any advantage you have by being in a lowly populated area," Fin said. "As soon as one starts singing, the net tightens and they rush in. They're not your only concern either, you'll have to deal with hungry humans too. Conscience has a terrible habit of only returning after your belly's full. Hunger can make you do unspeakable things."

"Any whiskey left?" Jack asked. "I could do with a drink. Actually, I could do with several."

Fin poured him one. "Eilish, I still want to hear the end of your story."

"Now?"

Fin nodded towards Ian, who still seemed a little

despondent at the knowledge he may have inadvertently harmed somebody.

"Right." Eilish took out a flask from her pack. From the face she pulled after a swig, Fin assumed it was not water. "We had no idea what was going on. I'm sure a lot of you can imagine. The worst storm to hit Ireland in over a decade and we had just met our first weeper."

5

A SHADE OF TURQUOISE

Candlelight flickered across the shelves, drawing the deranged stranger's stare.

"Is he okay?" Grace whispered.

"It's the full moon," Matthew said. "All the crazies are out tonight."

The man lost interest and started moving along the glass. Eilish wished there was something more substantial separating them. She shined the torch directly in his face. He did not flinch or blink, but he started to weep.

Grace let out a hollow whimper. The man's hair was matted to his deathly pale forehead. His clothes were muddy, ruined and torn. Buttons were missing from his blood-stained shirt. His mouth opened and closed awkwardly. The sound of his weeping was so gut-wrenching and irregular that Matthew moved towards the door to open it.

"Don't you dare," Grace said. "Look at him."

Eilish could see no sign of grief or pain on his face to match the weeping. His expression was serene, almost like a sleepwalker having a nightmare.

Matthew stepped back. The movement riled the man and he collided with the window. The entire pane shuddered.

Derek took the torch from Eilish and turned it off. Matthew knocked the candles over in his haste to put them out. They stood in darkness and watched as the man tried the window again. Behind him, a car pulled into the station. The headlights illuminated bloody handprints streaked across the glass.

The man's bloodshot eyes fixed on each of them in turn. He dashed forward. The impact staggered and turned him around enough to notice the car by the pumps. The driver had forgotten to turn the wipers off beneath the garage shelter. Their frantic whumping against the dry windshield caused enough noise to make the driver ignorant of the sick man. Eilish ran to the window and knocked as hard as she could. The driver sped off. The sick man followed. He seemed unsure on his feet, stumbled on the road and fell.

He vanished until another car came to a skidding halt a few feet in front of him. Headlights saturated the prone man with an unnatural glow. The driver only hesitated for a moment. The tires squealed. When the car struck him, it juddered and rose as the man went beneath the wheels. The driver only slowed enough to keep control.

"Call an ambulance!" Frank was shaking so much that he struggled to unlock the door. Eilish followed him into the night and was quickly soaked by the storm.

The man was still alive, staring blankly into the boiling, black clouds. Seeing his mangled form was like a searing rod through Eilish's mind. She wanted to help, but knew nothing could be done. She assumed his back was broken by the way his pelvis was turned at such an extreme angle. There was a concave dip in his chest where some of his ribs had been crushed. His shirt had been torn off. No sound came out of his moving mouth. *At least he does not seem conscious of the pain.*

Matthew stumbled to the ditch at the side of the road and vomited. Nobody spoke. They did not know what to say.

Eilish was the first to notice the wailing behind the wind. "What's that?"

"Alarms?" Grace said.

"I hear screaming." Matthew wiped his mouth with his sleeve and retched again.

Derek blessed himself. "Can you hear weeping?"

A flashing blue light illuminated the countryside. The siren of a Garda car was muffled by the storm. It looked as if it would slow down and pull into the garage, but when the driver saw them, the engine revved and the wheels skidded across the wet surface. The horn blared. They just managed to get out of the way before the dying man was run over again. The meaty echo of a human head striking tarmac was enough to cause Eilish to double over and puke. Mercifully, the man no longer moved. The Garda stopped down the road. Steam rose off the bonnet. He watched them through the rear-view mirror. After a few tense moments, he rolled down the window. "Is the garage open?"

The question was so casual that it threw Eilish. "You just killed a man."

"Was he crying?"

"He was acting strange," Derek said.

"Then I did you a favour. Are the pumps working?"

"Power's out," Eilish said.

He cursed. "Stay away from him. Get inside, I'll follow you in." His radio chirped incessantly. His uniform demanded compliance. The handcuffs and baton were there should further incentives be required.

A Ring of Oak & Apple

He parked as close to the shop door as possible. There was a manic, half-crazed glaze to his face. Before saying a word, he checked the aisles were clear with his torch. "Does Jess still have the generator out back?"

When Eilish realised he was talking to her, she hurried to fill the silence. "Yes, it should have kicked in when the power went out. But it's not for the fuel pumps, just the freezers."

"Good. I'll get an electrician down here to sort it out. We need that fuel. No good to us there." He wiped at his pale face. Eilish thought he was soaked from the storm, but beads of sweat had started to gather on his skin again.

"What in the hell is going on? Are you just going to leave that lad out there on the road?" Matthew asked.

"Savour your ignorance. I wish it was only me that went mad. Suppose you wouldn't have caught the news without the power." He stopped speaking, put up a hand in a sign for patience and vomited acidic-smelling bile. "Sorry about that."

Derek took a bottle of water from the fridge and handed it to him. The guard downed half of it. "Have any of you been bitten, or had much contact with people like your man out there?"

Their look of confusion was enough of an answer for him.

Grace stood at the window, transfixed by the body. *Better that he died. Imagine living in that state.* Eilish admonished herself for that thought.

Matthew paced, his face illuminated by the light of his phone. "There's government warnings about a disease. Doesn't say anything about running people down in the street!"

"Keep your voice low. I don't have long. I used the siren

to draw them away from town. I'm sorry to say, there's a crowd coming your way. Still doesn't seem real. They'll not show you what I saw on the news – there's too much of it. Dublin, Galway, they're gone. I don't know what it is. Cities are war zones. Whole country..." The words caught in his throat. "I'm just after witnessing... I don't know. Managed to lock some in the care home. Kept others in the church. Couldn't tell the sick from the terrified. God help me, but we locked them all in just the same." He trembled.

Martin put his high-visibility vest on, as if wearing it brought his mind some clarity. "I need to get home."

"You're English?" the garda asked. "Hunker down here. Unless you're swimming, you're not getting off this island."

Eilish held herself. "What are we supposed to do?"

"Put up the barriers out front. I don't want anybody coming near those pumps. I'm taking charge of them. Anybody gives you trouble, give it right back. Pull the shutters down over the windows and stay quiet. This place should be okay, so long as you don't draw their attention."

"Then what?" Matthew asked.

"Wait for the army. Beyond that, I don't know." The garda pinched the bridge of his nose. Sweat poured from his skin despite the cold. "Half the roads are flooded. River through town has burst its banks. Trees down. Power's out. I'd love nothing more than to fill my tank and keep driving. Don't think I could get far enough."

"How can we help?" Derek asked.

"I'll send people your way. Just look after them." He went through the aisles with a shopping basket and filled it with batteries, water and latex gloves. "You might want to try making masks to cover your faces. Cover any cuts as well. We don't know anything, but if this isn't biblical, then it spreads fast through contact, or possibly the air."

"Should we find weapons to defend ourselves?" Derek asked.

The garda considered it. "They're too fast and wild. Better off keeping quiet. Now, do any of you have first aid training?" Before he got an answer, he took his jacket off and put a kit onto the counter.

"No, but I'm not squeamish," Derek said.

"Right, patch me up as best you can." Dark blood made the blue shirt stick to his back. He unbuttoned and winced as it peeled away from the wound.

Derek made a sound which made Eilish wonder if he was lying about not being squeamish. Deep gouges cut into the flesh of his shoulder and neck. The skin around the wound was flaming red and glistening. The garda turned his flashlight on and handed it to Eilish. "Be quick. I've got work to do." He popped a few painkillers into his mouth and washed them down with water. His teeth chattered.

Eilish held the light, but looked away from the blood. Derek used tweezers to pull something out and held it close to the torch. It was a fingernail, painted a lovely shade of turquoise. Derek poured water over the wound, sprayed on antiseptic, and patched it up as best he could. By the end the garda had turned ghostly pale and shook so much that Eilish thought he would pass out.

"How did you get this?" Eilish asked.

"You know the woman who runs the tea shop in town?"

"Helen?"

"That nail belongs to her. It took two of us to stop her. She nabbed me just as we were closing the door. They all wept with this calm expression on their faces. It was maddening. I thought my skin was going to jump off my body."

He stood, flexed his shoulder and flinched. Derek had

made a poor job of it. Some of the skin had bunched up, pinched together by the stitches.

"Are you sure you're able to drive?" Grace asked.

"For now." He dressed and looked at his watch. "It'll be a long night. Good luck." He stopped at the door for a second before leaving.

Eilish was almost certain she saw him crying.

"Hang on," Martin said. "I'll drive you. You look like you're about to pass out."

"I'd appreciate it."

Martin looked as if he would say goodbye to them, but it seemed too final, so he just nodded instead and left.

The blue lights blazed silently as they pulled out onto the road. The wail of the siren made Eilish's breath catch. She ran to the door. "We have to get the shutters down and close the gates." She hesitated at the handle. It was smeared with blood. She used her elbow.

"I tried calling the emergency services," Grace said. "Goes to a recording."

"Derek, wash your hands. If he has it, we could get sick." Eilish's breathing was slow and shallow at the thought of being so close to the garda that she had felt heat rising from him. Could smell the tang of old cigarette smoke and ineffective deodorant.

Derek just stopped himself before touching his face. "Had it not been for the wound on his back, I'd've thought he was mad. No, sorry, I still think he's mad, but he didn't do that to himself." He pointed to the nail on the counter. "We'll do as he said, but we're not staying here. We'll all fit in the cab of my truck. Take what we need and hide until it's over."

"This seems like somebody is pulling a prank on us," Matthew said.

Derek held up his bloody hands. "If somebody is willing to go to this much effort to trick us, then I suggest we play along."

6

LAST CUSTOMER

In all her time at the garage, Eilish had never seen the shutters pulled down. They had not been oiled in years and their shrieking, as they were worried out of their casings, set the nerves in her teeth to shivering. The storm would dilute the noise, but she still felt eyes in the dark on them.

Matthew, Grace and Eilish worked on separate shutters. Frank filled baskets with food and carried packets of water out to his truck. Derek had just locked the first barrier at the entrance to the garage when a car coming from town crashed into it. It was a glancing blow. The driver struggled against a deflating airbag to get out. Weeping came from the back seats. The driver looked like he was about to attack Derek, until he yelled at him. The man visibly relaxed. *Was he expecting him to weep?* Ignoring Derek, he hopped over the barrier and went straight for the pump. "Have you any petrol cans?"

"There's no power," Eilish said. "They won't work."

The man picked up a nozzle and pulled the trigger. Nothing came out. He threw it on the ground with a curse and returned to his car. The wipers were stuck against the shattered windshield. The only thing restraining the weepers in the back of the car were their seatbelts.

"Do you need help?" Grace asked.

That brought the man back to some semblance of reality. "I think I've enough petrol to get them to hospital." He spoke as if trying to reassure himself. The closed car door did not muffle the sound of weeping, it grew louder and busier, like a choir of keeners surrounding the station. When he drove away, somebody ran from the shadows, trailing his tail lights, right past Derek.

Eilish felt the strength leave her legs. She grabbed Grace's arm to steady herself. The only light came from the car. *They can't see us.* Derek hid behind the barrier. He waved for them to get inside the shop.

The car stopped. Its high beams illuminated a crowd of people shuffling down the road. It was a scene lifted from a nightmare. Young, old, fit and feeble, all of them wept.

They rushed towards the light. Some stumbled and fell in their haste and were trampled. The engine roared when they swarmed the car. Nobody moved out of the way. Some were knocked aside. Others disappeared under the wheels. The light was swallowed by the sheer number of bodies. One of the infected went over the roof, sliding across the slick metal. His body broke the already weakened windshield.

Where are they all coming from? The car was surrounded, but the driver blindly pushed on. Derek quickly crawled towards them. They fled back inside the garage. Two windows remained unshuttered. To try to pull them down now would only draw the infected.

Matthew leaned against the glass door. "Only one of the barriers is closed."

Grace braced the door too. "What are we supposed to do? What the hell is wrong with them?"

"Where's Frank?" Derek asked. His whole front was black with dirt.

They heard an engine start up at the back of the yard.

"He's leaving us." Matthew was frantic.

They watched as Frank's speed camera van quietly rolled towards the gate.

"I know what he's up to." Derek moved them aside and ran towards the gate. He closed it just as Frank wedged his van against it. The darkness was alive with squirming, weeping silhouettes, like a ghoulish procession of mourners.

The gate swung ahead of the van and banged against the bollard. The sound of reverberating metal took some of the attention off the car. With little use left in caution, Frank wedged the van against the barrier and put the break on. The infected rushed the front of the van.

Derek opened the back door just as Frank tumbled out, landing hard on the ground.

"Run!" Grace roared as the infected toppled over the low wall into the garage grounds.

"What did you shout for? I wasn't dawdling," Derek said as Matthew slammed the door shut behind him and Frank.

"I got a glimpse down the road," Frank said. "We can't stay here. Half the town's out there."

"Out the back way," Derek said. "The truck's high enough off the ground. We'll be safe there."

Infected reached the windows. The darkness inside the garage kept them hidden from the wandering eyes of the weepers.

"Grab as much food as you can," Frank whispered.

* * *

A Ring of Oak & Apple

Eilish worried about all the cleaning she was going to have to do after all of this was over. They gathered in the back room, the smell of bleach making her head ache. Frank opened the door while the others stood ready to rush it, should any infected try get in. "It's clear."

He stepped into the storm, not giving them time for second guessing. *Don't get left behind.* She knew if she was alone when this started, she would just have curled up behind the counter. Their escape was cloaked by the heavy rain. Puddles were massing into ponds and the usually quiet gurgle of the drainage ditch behind the garage now sounded like rapids.

Spiked metal fences surrounded the car park. *We're trapped.*

Eilish heard the infected clambering over the car that had stalled on the road. *If not for them, we'd all be dead right now.* A growing number of alarms haunted the night. *How widespread is this?*

Derek opened the door of the truck and lifted the bags of food in before helping the others up. Grace pulled the curtain of the cabin back and sat on the bed. Eilish took the passenger's seat beside Frank, while Derek sat behind the wheel. Eilish felt like she could not breathe properly until the door was closed.

"We're not all going to fit," Matthew said.

"You're welcome to wait in your own van," Derek said.

"Does the TV work?" Grace asked.

They all crammed into the back of the cab to look at the small screen. Before turning it on, Derek unplugged his neon Liverpool sign. News played on all the channels. It did not matter which station he tuned into, they all said the same thing: Ireland was under attack.

"I can't get through to my wife," Frank said.

A government warning flashed across the screen, becoming more apocalyptic as the night progressed.

* * *

Storm Peggy caused the cab to rock on its suspension. Eilish imagined the motion was from senseless infected trying to get in. Nobody slept. When sunlight peeked through the partition in the curtains, Eilish pulled them back. Derek rolled down his window and listened. There was the patter of a light rain, the chirp of a few disgruntled birds, but no weeping. They were gone.

"What do we do now?" Grace was the first to speak, breaking the hours-long silence.

There was no answer.

The television was still on. There was too much horror on display; Eilish was numb to it. *We're on our own. They're not people any more. This is the end of the world.*

"Do we kill ourselves?" Matthew asked. Eilish could not figure out by his tone if he was joking or not. Grace got sick in the wastebasket. Eilish rolled down her window to let in crisp morning air.

A timid knock on the door made them jump. *Can infected open doors?* Derek looked down and let out a laugh, the first genuine one since giving Frank the speed stripes for his van.

"It's your favourite customer Eilish."

Eilish leaned over him to look.

"Hello dear."

"Phyllis, what – how?"

"Any chance of getting a few scratch cards?"

"Have you not heard the news?" Eilish asked.

"I have, but I can't believe it. I was told to come here. The place was empty and my Charles, rest his soul, he used to drive trucks, so I thought I'd check the cabs for survivors."

"Is there anybody else?" Eilish felt ashamed for having left her post when the garda asked for their help.

"No. I thought I was alone. I tried knocking on doors. Neighbours I've known since they were children cursed me to leave them be. Then there were houses with the sound of weeping inside. I stopped calling after that."

"How did you get through the roads?" Grace asked. "They were full of the infected last night."

"The sirens drew them away. The sergeant mentioned that him and two of his officers were going to lure them off. They told everybody to stay inside or come here. Then the three of them went to the hills around town and blared their sirens throughout the night."

Eilish could picture them. Not locals, but they integrated well. There was Mark with a head of coarse ginger hair and Charlotte, known affectionately as Rottweiler around town. *She's younger than me. They spent the night helping people, while we hid.*

"Any room in there for me?" Phyllis asked. "It's just – I don't want to walk back. I don't think I can go home."

Derek got out and stretched. "It's not safe here."

"Want my advice?" Phyllis said. "Load up all you can, everything of use from the vans and shop. Then head into the countryside before the roads get any worse."

They had discussed that very thing during the night, but nobody really knew what to do. Phyllis's news was the decider, they could not stay so close to town. The truck seemed the best option as it fit them all. Derek was mostly hauling commercial packages: fabrics, metals, wood and a few boxes for pharmacies – nothing of much use to them now – so they detached the trailer.

Eilish, Phyllis and Frank went into the store to take as much food as they could. The infected had not made it inside. The windows were so badly marred by their filth that it dulled the light of the morning sun.

"This feels wrong," Eilish said. "What about the rest of the people in town?"

Phyllis unspooled all of the scratch cards from the stand and stuffed them in her pockets. "Nobody will come here, it's too close to town. Just worry about us. Do you want a few lottery tickets dear?"

"I don't think they'll be running the draw, Phyllis."

"Machine's down anyway. Pity."

* * *

Apart from a few downed branches, the road was mostly clear. *It should have been a quiet day. What would I be doing right now? Getting ready for bed, probably.* Eilish realised that there was nothing she needed to return to her apartment for. The plants were plastic, they would keep.

The cab of the truck quickly filled and became cramped. It would be an uncomfortable squeeze, but safe. Eilish left the garage doors unlocked and put the keys on the counter. Part of her still wondered if this was an overreaction. She laughed at the thought that she might lose her job. *If there are survivors in town, who am I to stop them from getting a bit to eat?*

Phyllus rifled through some of the crumpled tickets beside the lottery machine. "What's the matter with these?"

"Nothing," Eilish said. "Somebody might change their mind when they get a look at the quick pick numbers or want another line added on. I just leave them there."

Phyllus took most of them for herself, but gave one to

Eilish. "Never know, could be on to a winner with that one, when they start doing the draws again."

My lucky ticket. It was strange, she did not want to leave it behind. Keeping it meant there was some kind of hope that there would be another draw.

Matthew and Grace went through their haulage to find anything of use. They added heavy, all-weather jackets, first aid kits and nutritional bars to the store in Derek's truck.

"That's my job gone anyway," Matthew said.

"Were you watching different news to us?" Grace asked. "We're all unemployed now."

Frank opened the gate and hurried back to the truck. Eilish poured half a bottle of disinfectant into his cupped hands. Crows gathered on the powerlines, eyeing up the corpses on the road.

Derek took a deep breath, held it and exhaled as he started the truck. The noise meant they were now committed. Eilish wondered after the columns of smoke rising from town. Her father was terrible with technology, he rarely responded to her messages. Now was no different.

Matthew suggested a farm where he made deliveries. It was secluded, in the middle of nowhere, the perfect place to come up with a better plan. He would guide Derek through the winding lanes. The front of Frank's van was smeared with dirty copper streaks. Rain had washed the worst of it away. Derek tried to avoid the bodies, but there were too many. Eilish bit the hem of her sleeve and closed her eyes as the truck juddered.

The cabin towered above the hedges either side of the road, the countryside was as empty as it usually was. Eilish turned the radio on to distract them, but Derek quickly turned the news off at the mention of death tolls.

"Don't pay any attention to the bodies. Focus on the route," Derek said.

Tears streamed down Matthew's face. "Turn right and then left at the next junction."

The car that had been swarmed during the night was now half-sunk into the ditch. The front seat was empty.

Eilish bit her tongue to stop from suggesting they turn back.

They encountered a few speeding cars coming from the opposite direction. A few beeped from behind to overtake. *Nobody knows where to go.* Derek stopped at the brow of a hill and got out. Eilish followed when he gave the all clear. She climbed onto the top of the truck to survey the town. It was difficult to make out the flashing blue lights of the Garda cars during daytime, but she spotted them all. Lighthouses drawing the storm to them.

Thank you.

7

NEIGHBOURLY

Eilish was quiet for some time before people realised her story had ended. "Why am I doing all the talking? This circle jerk is too one-sided. How did you end up here?"

Jack became awkward with the sudden attention. "Not much to tell." He sat up out of his slouch and wrapped his musty blanket tighter around him. "I was working in Dublin at the time of the outbreak."

"You're the first person I've spoken to that came from the capital," Fin said.

It piqued the interest of everybody in the circle, bar the man hunkered close to the fire. He had stopped shivering, but had not engaged with anybody yet.

"Hang on, don't start without me," a woman said. She disappeared from the light and warmth of the circle and headed towards the shore. She returned with a case of beer. "Left them cooling away from the fire."

"There goes the early start tomorrow," Eilish said, rubbing her hands together as she eagerly helped open the crate.

The bottles made a cheerful clanging sound as they

were passed around. Somebody attempted to open the cap with their teeth, evoking collective outrage.

"Are you mad?" Jack asked. "You do realise that there aren't any dentists about? And you'd be lucky to find a pair of ice-skates in Ireland to do a *Cast Away* job on it."

Eilish threw a bottle opener to the culprit. "I thought the psychopath was just an overused thrope in post-apocalyptic films. Never thought I'd encounter a maniac."

"I heard a dentist set up shop in one of the abandoned military camps," somebody said. "They have power for their drills and enough numbing stuff to give half of Ireland fillings. That's where I'm heading."

"Are your teeth at you that much that you'd risk your life over them?" Eilish asked.

"Not now, but if this thing spreads, then there won't be any dentists left."

"I was terrified of the dentist," Fin said. "Haven't had a reason to go in years, but I'd near follow you to that camp to get my teeth checked." He took the bottle opener and revelled in the hiss as he popped the cap. "That's easily the best beer I've ever had," he said after savouring the first long drink.

"It's the company that makes it," Eilish said.

Fin sat forward, resting his elbows on his knees. "To lost company." He raised his bottle in a toast before taking a drink to push down the bile rising in his throat. There was no longer any pleasure in it. *It does not do any good to dwell on what is gone.*

While wondering whom the sombre-faced amongst them were drinking to, his thoughts were interrupted by choking sounds coming from the tent with the new arrival inside.

Fin had his hammer in his hand before he gained his

feet. The other survivor by the fire cowered at the commotion. *He knows something.* "Check him," Fin said, while he approached the tent with Eilish and Jack. Each of them put their masks back on. It hurt the bruised skin around his mouth, but it meant less chance of infection. Eilish wielded a knife and Jack had a shovel.

"Jack, if he rushes us, you try to keep him back with the business end of your shovel. We'll try to take him to the ground."

"Why take the chance?" Eilish said. "Just use your pistol."

Fin shook his head. "Surrounding hills are like an amphitheatre. The sound would draw too many." *I can't risk getting stuck again.*

The crying seemed different to the weeping of the infected. They listened as the man tried to control it. Hold it in and stifle the anguish, but it seeped past his resolve to contain it.

"Are you okay?" Eilish asked.

There was silence as the whole camp listened. A log split in the fire, making Fin tighten his grip on the hammer. *Silence means he has not turned.*

"I don't want to die. I'm not okay. I think I'm infected."

Behind them, the other survivor was stripped down to his underwear. He struggled beneath the weight of somebody kneeling on his back. Fin cursed. No amount of alcohol could numb him for what needed to be done now.

"Get out Alan, they're going to kill you if you don't!" The other survivor said.

Somebody struck him a horrible blow to the back of the head with a thick walking stick. Not enough to cause lasting damage, but it kept him quiet out of fear of worse.

Everybody stepped back when the zip of the tent

shrieked and Alan came out. His eyes were red, almost painfully inflamed. *He could mourn for all the dead in Ireland and still his eyes would not look so raw.* There was no question about it, the man was lost. Fin felt an odd sense of relief, like he was now absolved for what was about to happen.

Tears streaked Alan's face and thick, milky snot trickled from his nose, a thread of it connected his parted lips as he whimpered. "I don't want to die."

He was much younger than Fin. *He should be in college in a lecture hall or dawdling with friends.* Sympathy at the situation was quickly boiled away by anger that colleges across the country would be devoid of the living. *How long until people can go back to the way things were? When can I sit in a pub and raise a glass to the horrors of the epidemic and toast its end? How long will I keep thinking there's anything to go back to?*

"What makes you think you're infected?" Eilish asked. By the way she held her knife, Fin knew she was certain too.

Alan trembled. He opened his jacket, turned his back to them and pulled up his jumper. There was a scrape just above his belt. The skin around the injury was bright red. Alan flinched when the fabric of his jumper grazed it. The scrape looked like something he would have barely felt. *He probably thought he had escaped. Poor bastard. If only they had gotten him, instead of giving him false hope and leaving us to deal with this.*

Alan gauged their reactions. What little composure he retained shattered. He seemed frail now, as if he knew that he was on his own now until the end.

"I don't want to die."

"Might just be anxiety," Fin lied and hated himself for it. "We don't know how this virus works. Though, let's get you away from others, just to be sure. Cover your mouth. Zip up your jacket and we'll wait it out on the shore."

A Ring of Oak & Apple

Alan nodded and did everything asked of him. He was complacent, glad to have somebody else giving the orders. Fin, Eilish and Jack followed him across uneven ground away from the camp. The air behind Fin's mask was warm and his breath smelled foul. Alan no longer tried to fight back his sobs. He covered his mouth through his mask to muffle the sound.

It was too dark between the trees for Fin to make out the faces of the others. The pace was slow, they all knew what had to be done. *Who cuts away another part of their soul tonight?*

Alan stopped at the water's edge and looked towards the land. "My parents are still out there, somewhere."

No they're not.

Eilish broke ranks first and sat on the eroded bank. She patted the ground for Alan to sit. "How did you survive this long? Don't be insulted, but you seem so very green."

Alan sat down hard, making him huff. Fin kept his distance. The air around Alan could be laced with whatever caused this.

"We had more food in the house than we usually would. It was my family's turn to host Christmas. They were away when it happened. Last time I spoke to them over the phone they told me to hunker down and wait. It was me, Josh – the guy in camp – and a few others. We were okay for a couple of weeks, but Shane was sick of waiting. Took more than his fair share and went out looking for his fiancé. He knew we wouldn't try going after him. Yesterday was the first time I left the house. Even if we still had the food, I don't think a few more months' worth would see us through this."

"Sadly, I think you're right," Fin said.

Somebody from the camp snuck out of the woods with a crowbar and what was left in the bottle of whiskey. They offered both to Fin out of sight of Alan, before slinking back between the trees. The crowbar was heavy in his hands. It seemed an ugly weapon, but he needed something that he could swing with enough force that Alan would not feel a thing. He hid it in the rocks on the shore and approached with the whiskey.

Alan took the bottle and cradled it in his arms. "Ah man." He looked up to the stars to try hold back fresh tears. "There's so much I wanted to do and I'm only now realising that I wanted to do it."

Most of the people Fin met that were infected, but still conscious, gave in to this morbid nostalgia for a life they would never get to live. Survivors seemed to bury those thoughts, block them away as a sort of poisonous hope. *To think about what could have been lets dread seep in. No, not just dread, it's indifference that's the killer.*

Ian joined them from his patrol of the island. It did not take him long to understand the situation, or he had been listening from the shadows all along. "Do you want to write a letter to your family? I've paper and a pen," he said.

Alan considered it for a moment and nodded. The act seemed grim, like digging your own grave, or etching your headstone. The words came slowly at first, but after a few sentences, his handwriting became sloppy from the speed with which he wrote.

Fin left them to return to his kayak. He dug into the bottom to retrieve a packet of plastic page protectors. His hand rested on his rifle as he wondered about using it to ease Alan's passing. Nobody in the clearing spoke, they stared into the fire, each in their own personal hell, hoping that they would not be called upon. *This must be how a teacher felt when they asked a question of the class.* Alan's friend looked at him with unbridled rage.

"Josh, do you want to speak with Alan?" Fin asked.

Josh shook his head; the look on his face was a mix of horror, rage and desperation.

Fin left the rifle. A kindness for one would endanger all and he did not have the bullets for that much mercy. He brought the page protector back to Alan who was reading over his letter. Alan put the tip of the pen against the page as if he would write more. *Say all you want, run the ink dry, it will change nothing.*

Fin went to pick up the crowbar, but Ian put a hand on his shoulder and absolved him of the murder. With thick gloves Fin took from his kayak, he held Alan's hand. He could feel the fingers spasming, trying to close so that the fingernails could dig into the palm. Jack took the letter.

Trying to stop the weeping seemed to cause Alan considerable pain. He gagged and choked, biting off sobs. "Eilish – how did your story end?"

She stood in front of him to hold his attention. Fin realised that Alan was not aware that they had taken up positions to hold him down if needed. Fin heard the quiet grating of the metal crowbar against shorestones. His own anxiety flared at the thought of Ian, a stranger, holding a deadly weapon behind him. He leaned slightly away from Alan.

"Where did I leave off?" Eilish said.

"You were all in the truck heading out of town."

"Oh yeah." She was silent for a time. "I often wondered after the Gardaí that used their sirens to lure the infected away from town. Sometimes I dream that I'm in a squad car with no escape and I know I've to put the sirens on, but I never can. Whether it was bravery, or they were not completely sure of the consequences, through their actions, I'm alive."

Alan was rapt in Eilish's story, he paid no attention to the quiet approach of Ian.

"We made it to…"

Ian let out a grunt as he swung the crowbar and brought it down on Alan's head with such force that life left him. Fin felt his hand spasm and squeeze his own before going limp. He turned his head for fear of blood spatter. Alan fell face first onto the shore. Eilish, Jack and Fin stepped away as Ian raised the crowbar and brought it down a few more times to ensure Alan would not suffer for long.

A few birds were unsettled by the noise and took flight. Now that the deed was done, Fin felt his anxiety ebb away. They stood still and quiet for a few respectful moments. The body spasmed, reminding Fin of days spent fishing with his father, when he anointed the fish with a heavy blow. Death was different now. The dead could no longer suffer and they could do no harm to the living. So long as it kept happening to others, he could live with that.

"Move back," Ian said to them. He turned Alan's head to the side, ensured his mask and goggles were in place and forced the sharp end of the crowbar down through the temple, destroying the brain. He worried it free and ran the end through the icy lake water. "Stick it in the fire when you get back, no point wasting any of the bleach when we have fire."

"Thank you for doing that," Fin said.

Ian shrugged. "Somebody had to and you're a guest. No time to rest. Let's get the other lad out of the way."

"If he's infected," Jack added.

Ian put the arms of the body behind its back and locked them together with a zip tie. He did the same to the legs. "Don't want to take any chances," he said. "We can dispose of him in the morning."

"What will we do with his letter?" Jack asked.

"You're holding the last bit of a man's soul left on this earth," Ian said. "We'll keep it safe with ours."

Fin reflected on his lack of queasiness as they walked back to the camp. Already the habitual passage of people had worn a trail through the undergrowth. *Am I numb to killing?* Whatever it was, he did not let himself dwell on it for long. He put it down to relief that Alan could do no harm now. *He wrote his letter, he got more than most.* Fin pressed a hand to his chest where his own letter lay nestled in an inside pocket. He added to it when it was safe to do so and he was sober enough. It was becoming a journal of sorts. Something to talk to in isolation.

There was a commotion in the camp. When they entered the clearing the fire made Fin night blind. As his vision returned, he stared down the dark chasm of his own rifle.

8

GHOST IN A BOTTLE

"You killed him!" Flecks of spittle flew when Josh spoke. He let out a guttural, desperate moan through gritted teeth. He spun on the spot, trying to keep everybody under watch, but he kept bringing the rifle back to point squarely at Fin.

Not many people in Ireland knew more about guns than what they learned from television, movies and games. Though there was no science to pulling the trigger.

"He was sick," Fin said. "You knew, didn't you? And you said nothing." He only noticed Jack and Eilish at his sides. He heard rustling behind him and wondered if Ian was trying to get a better vantage on Josh, or get out of range.

"You don't know that. Even if he was, you didn't give him a chance. There could be a cure!"

"There might be," Jack said. "But it would be too late for any of us. He was sick. Nobody here could deny it. What we did was kindness. He didn't suffer." Jack shrank away from the muzzle of the rifle now pointed at him.

"Kindness with a crowbar? You'll do the same to me. Keep your good intentions." The man spat towards him.

"You're a fool!" Anger got the better of Fin. Enraged that

anybody could be so clueless as to spit around a group of people during an epidemic. "If you're sick, then you might infect others. I don't begrudge you hiding away while the rest of the country died. No harm in it. I should have done the same. But you can't be so stupid or indifferent to others, that you would spit."

"I'm not sick."

Fin looked to the others in the group. "There's not a scratch on him," a woman said. "But if his friend was infected… could be, that the virus was passed another way."

"I'm not sick! Take it back." Josh roared and turned the gun on her. She shrank away.

Beneath the trees behind Josh a flashlight turned on. It was enough of a distraction to draw his attention. Fin rushed forward and tackled him. Fear bolstered Josh's strength, and he used Fin's momentum to swing him off. If not for Eilish and Jack tackling him too, he would have lost. Fin kicked the rifle aside and was about to join the scuffle when Josh spat, using the only weapon he had left.

Fin noticed his kayak had been turned out. All of his possessions spilled across the cold ground.

Josh stood up and spat on his hands, rubbing the saliva along his arms. "I'm leaving on that kayak. Let me go and you'll not have to worry about me."

"You're not taking anything of mine," Fin said. "You don't have to go. Your friend has passed, believe me, I know what you're going through. You're full of rage and want to lash out. Nobody here thinks any less of you. Let it be over, let this be forgotten. We're all friends now. Please – don't make us enemies. You've lost someone, we all have. Relax. Sit by the fire and we'll have a drink."

"If you want to be alone, you can have my tent," Eilish said. "There are blankets in there and we've batteries for a video player. You could watch a movie. Take your mind off things."

Josh looked to the crowbar they used to kill Alan. *That was indelicately done.*

"Just let him go," somebody urged. "The weepers are listening to all of this."

"Take one of the rafts," another said.

Fin put up his hand to quiet them. "You don't need to leave. You're not a prisoner. The shore is crawling with weepers. They'll spot you in the moonlight. If you want to leave in the morning, I've food I can give you and I'll drop you on the shore." Fin watched the man's face jitter from one expression to another as he raced through different emotions. *Maybe he wants to die. Death by survivor is better than death by weeper. No, why conceal weapons? He wants to live.*

"I'm taking the kayak, the food and the supplies in it. What are you going to do about it?" Josh said with scorn. "There's not a bit of muscle on you." People moved out of the way as he approached with saliva-covered hands. Their fear and apprehension only encouraged him. Josh looked Fin up and down and the result was a snide grin. He approached him with his shoulders raised, trying to look bigger than he actually was. "What are you going to do about it, yeah? Come on, do something, yeah." His face contorted as he tried to keep that derisive grin going.

Fin imagined the act must have worked before for Josh to use it now. Josh started wailing in a mockery of the weepers cry.

Posturing was just a game. Like cats yowling, squaring off and raising their hackles. Trying to do as much as they could to avoid a fight, both knowing neither would come away unscathed. Fin had no time for games.

Josh put his hands up towards Fin's face. Fin did not budge, but he trembled with a rage so intense that it boiled away any sympathy he had for the man. Josh stepped closer, about to touch him. "What are you going to do about it–"

Before he could get another 'yeah' in, Fin drove the hilt of his knife into Josh's groin. He let out a pained guffaw. Fin turned the edge of the blade away from his body just in case Josh tried to push it in. Fin grabbed onto him as he doubled over and used his weight to bring him down. He had never really grappled before and for a moment he worried he had inadvertently given Josh the advantage. But the sight of the blade had cowed him.

Fin knelt over him. A knee on one arm, the other on his chest. The sharp edge of the knife pressed against Josh's neck. There was no more bravado, just a petrified human that had lost everything, waking every day into an endless nightmare.

The adrenaline put a tremble in Fin's voice. "You think you're a hard man, do you? You're some boy, I'll tell you that. This is what's going to happen now. You make a move or piss me off and I'll take the easiest option. I'll whip this knife along your neck. I've seen it done before. Doesn't seem to look too sore. Though, that could be the mind preoccupied with other things. People start wondering 'Am I actually dying? Is this really the end?' The very thought would raise the heartbeat of anyone. Not a good thing when you've an artery open. Though your brain already seems starved of oxygen. You might get away with it."

"Come on, he's had enough." Somebody stepped forward as if to intervene.

"I'm not here to make friends," Fin said. "I hate being interrupted. You sit down. Not a thing is going to happen to this little fellow. His future's in his hands. Now boy. We're not going to fight with fists. That's completely daft. What happens if, say, you break a knuckle or a finger? Forbid the notion of getting a cut and an infection. Not these days. So I'll use my knife. Now, I'll be completely honest with you. I don't think I did a thorough job cleaning it the last time I gutted a weeper. It's not like I use it to clean my teeth."

Josh went pale. He was malleable now to any suggestion that would get the possibly infected knife away from him. Fin pressed it closer to his skin and he stopped breathing.

"Should you insist on fighting, I'm no surgeon, so I'd only be guessing. I'd try not to hit anything vital. But would that be a kindness? Leaving you to die of infection or bleed out slowly? A quick death would be the neighbourly thing to do. Maybe I should aim for a lung, or try to get it between the ribs into the heart. As I said, it's all guesswork to me. Or you could stop your tantrum, sit by the fire and have a beer. What's it going to be? Are you going to behave?"

Josh shook so violently that Fin had to pull the knife away to a safe distance. He spoke so softly that Fin only knew he said 'yes' by the movement of his lips.

"I'm not your lover, lad, no need to whisper to me. Everybody's worried you're going to try to steal from them. Height of ignorance. People going hungry and you picking pockets. There are weepers and then below them in my estimation is scum that feels so privileged that they can take from others. It sickens me. Honestly, it would drive me to violence."

"I'll not take anything. I'm sorry."

Fin swallowed the lump in his throat. He felt bodily ill. *What am I doing?* He did not have a word for the look on Josh's face, but it would haunt him like all his other ghosts. He was breathing heavily, people must have thought he was building up to do the deed because Ian and Eilish started walking towards him. *These people don't know me. They're wary. They don't know my limits. May keep it that way. I don't want friends anymore.* Fin tossed the knife away and took Josh's hand to help him to his feet. "Friends it is. Does anybody have any bleach, I need to clean his spit off me."

Nobody offered. Fin went through his kayak, found a bottle. Poured some in Josh's trembling hands and went into the woods to clean himself. Once out of view of the others, he crouched behind a tree and vomited up the stew, whiskey and beer. *How many calories is that?* Eating was a daily chore, now he had to start again.

"Here."

Fin started. Ian stood behind him with a bottle of disinfectant.

"It's probably a little bit better for your skin than pouring bleach on yourself. Not by much though."

"Thank you."

Ian leaned against the tree. "You weren't going to kill him, were you?"

Fin gave a hollow laugh. "I was more likely to get sick on him than do that. I've seen good people do unspeakable things. Got me thinking that the only way you can be sure they won't hurt you, is to hurt them first."

"Why not kill them while you're at it?"

"The threat of death usually does the job. You saw yourself. I asked him to sit and think, but people just don't want to be rational."

"World's not rational anymore," Ian said.

Fin covered his skin in the disinfectant. The strong smell of alcohol robbed his nose of the earthy mix of ivy, moss and wet soil. "I hope I didn't go too far." He handed Ian the disinfectant.

"It's worrying me that I thought you didn't go far enough."

* * *

Back at camp Josh lay curled up by the fire, so close that the heat must have hurt. He covered his head with a blanket and flinched when he heard others come near. Nobody had touched Fin's things. *Maybe they worried I'd overreact.*

He was sure the sound of their argument had travelled across the lake to the infected. Fin packed his belongings as quietly as he could. He wondered if, in the silence of the camp, they might be able to hear his heart thumping.

His breath caught and the others were forgotten when he remembered Solene's perfume. Most of his things were accounted for except that. He rummaged through the grass looking for it. His hand glanced across the edge of the small glass bottle and he let out a long breath. It hid beneath a dock leaf. There was barely any left. Soon even the ghost of his girlfriend would be gone.

Fin checked everything twice, going over the items in his head. Aside from his death letter, and the perfume, the most important thing never left his person: the memory stick hanging around his neck. A few people in the camp took out bottles of toilet bleach and poured it on the ground where Josh had spat.

Eilish examined the rifle. "How did you come across this?"

Fin did not trust that his voice would not quiver if he spoke for any length of time. He sat with his back against the kayak. Despite his deep desire to, he did not spray the perfume. Having even the ghost of her in the bottle was a small hope that he could not lose. He held the cap close to his nose to breathe in the soothing smell.

"I was with a group of soldiers. What survivor hasn't become a magpie for useful things? It seemed too good to leave behind. I don't know. It's like a safety blanket. It brings me comfort knowing it's there."

"Much good against weepers?"

"If it was, it wouldn't be in my possession. If I remember, we were going clockwise and it was Jack's turn to tell us how the world ended for him."

"I don't think anybody is in the mood for hearing that," Jack said.

"People could do with a bit of cheering up, or a distraction."

Jack smiled. "There's nothing cheerful about what I've to say. I was in Dublin when shit hit the fan."

"The Pale?"

"It wasn't called that while I was there. I operated a tower crane right on the edge of the River Liffey. Made it my home for as long as I could. When did I know there was something wrong? When it was too late to do much about it."

9

FLYING THE NEST

'Tiredness Kills.' Jack's headlights illuminated the sign along the motorway. It gave him a jolt, wondering how he could barely remember the last hour of the journey. Tapping lightly on the brake, he brought his speed down to the legal limit. He had travelled most of the way to Dublin in a daze, without having to dip his high beams for oncoming traffic. A mix of coffee and energy drinks would keep him operational until he could sleep in his rented hostel bed that night.

Dublin was quiet and still. At this hour hangovers were only blossoming in the heads of late night revellers and the night shift workers were still hard at it. Tower cranes rose above the city skyline that they slowly shaped. Red aviation lights flickered at the top of the metal canopy. The tallest crane was where Jack was bound.

He parked on the building site and stretched after the long trip. A series of pops sounded up his spine. He joined the other sleepwalkers in the queue for the coffee van by the River Liffey. He watched as bleary lights came on in glass-fronted offices. Crews of cleaners set about making it look like yesterday never happened.

The wind channelling down the river was picking up speed. Here it only sent ripples across the water and aired out a few flags, but above the city – Jack looked up at the hulking, swaying cranes and felt his insides squirm.

With a thermos full of pitch-black coffee, he returned to the site. Other cars had fogged-up windows. *Lads pulling some serious overtime.* It did not bode well for his workload ahead. He underwent the usual test to ensure he was sober before starting the climb. Harsh electric lights illuminated the way through the concrete skeleton of what would become the elevator shaft. The night had not been cold enough for ice, but he still felt the chill through his heavy jacket and gloves. It took nearly twenty minutes to reach the cab. No matter how often he made the climb, the height always caused his insides to oscillate between tightening and churning. Broken eggshells, feathers and cigarette butts lined an old bird nest that he passed. The sight of the butts woke a craving in him that would not be sated for another twelve hours at least.

Hazy smoke drifted from chimneys. Steam vented off buildings. Amber, red and green traffic lights conducted the waking rituals of the city.

"Morning, Dublin." There were nearly a hundred cranes. He counted them on one of the slower days. Giants that lumbered over thousands of people, never fully considering how a river of steel, concrete and glass flowed right above them every day.

Inside the shelter of the cab, he blasted the heater up full. He sat into the cold cracked and sun-bleached seat and rested the hot thermos between his legs. The height never bothered him from here. He turned the radio on to listen to the morning news and ate his breakfast roll with the best view in the city.

"A red weather warning comes into effect this evening for Counties Galway, Mayo and Kerry. An orange warning is expected in the midlands." *So much for an easy day.*

In the distance the Wicklow Mountains dammed back dark rain clouds. The port was full of activity; a cruise ship docked while visitors explored the city and were robbed in Temple Bar by the price of a pint.

The city was alive long before the sun tinged the horizon. Commuters stuck in the congested arteries of the suburbs, all fitting into worn routines.

His work radio crackled into life. "Well Jack, how's the form?"

"My form depends completely on yours, Ronan. What side of the bed did you get out of this morning?"

"You assume I slept. There'll be none of that for either of us until this concrete pour is finished. There's forty lifts scheduled before then."

"Have you heard the weather reports?" Jack asked.

"Nothing we can do, but be careful. We'll lift until we can't. Same as always."

"Right, come on, I've a feeling this is as calm as the day's going to be."

Jack felt the pulse of the city quicken as the morning progressed. Vibrations from traffic, the building site below and the footfalls of countless people all hummed in his swaying cab. It was a humbling view, watching the ant colony in motion as he helped to extend it.

Ronan, his banksman, directed the first dozen lifts, his mood improving with each one. Glass, steel and cement took careful concentration to keep steady in spite of the wind. Just as they were getting into a productive rhythm, delays brought work to a standstill. An unprecedented number of accidents around the city had caused huge traffic delays. A development like this sitting idle cost thousands. The higher-ups would raise the blood pressure of those with radios to shout at everybody else. All Jack could do was watch and listen to the chaos unfolding.

The city became obscured by rain that fell so thick it sounded like it dented the crane. There seemed to be more blue flashing lights running through the maze than usual.

Jack called one of his friends in a crane closer to Grafton Street. "Lorcan, what's the story? What's going on your end?"

"How're things? Town's mad busy. Some accidents or something. Traffic goes on for as far as I can see. Take it things are quiet for you too."

"Nothing to do and the weather looks set to stay. Sitting here waiting on deliveries," Jack said. "Might be an early one. Last one to the pub pays for the first round."

"You're on. All I'm doing here is birdwatching. Though I don't mind getting paid to do it. My banksman is squealing up at me, but sure, I'm not driving the trucks," Lorcan said.

Nevan chimed in over the radio. "Apparently the motorway is a car park. Saw videos online about crashes. They had to close the Port Tunnel for a bit earlier too."

"Roads weren't slippery when I came in," Lorcan said. "Couple of lads never showed up for work this morning either. They put me with a lad from Belfast, I can't understand a word he's saying. May as well have no radio up here at all."

"Now that you mention it, half the lads haven't showed up for work here," Nevan said.

"Of all days for it. Probably just the holiday season," Jack said.

"Won't make for a happy New Year when they're given the boot. Plenty of other lads waiting to take their jobs," Lorcan said, with the experience of one who came to work sick to ensure he could keep paying his bills.

"All the nutters are out today. Some old, mad bastard bit me on the way in to work," Nevan said.

Jack frowned. "Did you say somebody bit you?"

"Yeah."

There was a brief pause before all of them started laughing.

"There'll be shots needed," Lorcan said.

"Yeah, I'll book a doctor's appointment. Don't worry."

"Wasn't you I was on about. Who knows what they caught off you."

"Probably long dead by now," Jack said.

"Hang on lads, I see cement trucks heading our way. Back to it." Lorcan ended the call.

Jack passed the message down to Ronan.

"We're in for a bastard of a day," Ronan said.

"What was the hold-up?"

"People not showing up. There's a bug doing the rounds and I can promise you, there are plenty that heard the news and jumped on the bandwagon to get a day off. Means more hours for us."

Jack cursed. "Let's make those millionaires even richer. It's not getting cosier up here with the weather."

"You good to go?"

"I've plenty of bottles for my home brew. May have to pinch a loaf before we finish, though."

"Stick a cork in it."

A Ring of Oak & Apple

* * *

Jack was exhausted long before the sun set. His concentration waned as artificial lights beamed up from below. The city was as beautiful at night as it was during the day. Its lights blurred to baubles by the rain on his window. The wind had become vicious by the time Ronan reluctantly called a halt to things.

"Leave the lock off the crane," Ronan said.

Jack did, allowing for the crane to move freely with the wind, essentially becoming a massive weathervane. The climb down was tense and terrifying. A protective cage ensured he could not fall far if he slipped. Bottles of cold piss sloshed about in his bag. Above him the wind took control of the crane.

"What's your plan?" Ronan asked when Jack reached the ground. He waited for him at the base of the crane.

"I'm not heading home. The roads seem lethal today."

"You're not staying in your car, are you?"

"Not a hope. There's more space in the crane and my back's in bits. I booked a hostel. Twenty euro for a shared room. Not bad, even if it does mean having to breathe the ass-tainted air of seven other people."

"I don't want you staying in a hostel."

"Well, I'm not spending money on a hotel, you must be joking. Not unless you're willing to give me a raise."

"Today is not the day to mention that. Stay at my place tonight. They've put me up in an apartment at the docklands. There's a spare room."

"You sure?" Jack asked.

"Absolutely. I had a go at a couple of lads calling in sick earlier, but then a few wives, partners and mothers started answering phones. The boys were too sick to pick up apparently. You remember Sully? Big man. If he said three words during the day, you'd think he was chatty."

"Yeah. Sound chap. Not like him to be out."

"I was on the phone to his wife earlier and heard him crying in the background." Ronan looked worried. "He finished a shift on site with a broken rib before, barely winced. Never thought I'd hear him weeping. Unsettled me something shocking."

"He was probably trying to sell it."

"Doubtful. That lad took to work like some of us would take to a holiday."

"You've only confirmed that he had mental illness. What do you reckon is doing the rounds?" Jack asked. "I've been listening to the news all day and can't seem to get a straight answer. Fair amount of elderly are dying from this. Might be a lockdown if it gets bad."

"Don't say that. We'll be out of work. I don't know what this is, but staying in a hostel strikes me as reckless at the moment."

"I'll take you up on the offer. Are you heading back with me?"

"Are you mad? I've a week's worth of work to finish before I can leave. Don't let me keep you." Ronan gave him the address, directions and the key. "There's plenty of food in the fridge. Help yourself to whatever you want. Don't go in somewhere to get dinner, don't even have it delivered. I'm deadly serious. If you get sick, I don't know what we'll do."

Jack put his headphones on and turned his hood up against the rain. A few taxis passed with their lights on. He was tempted, but did not fancy being cooped up again so soon. The other crane operators pulled out of drinks in the pub, worried that they would catch this sickness.

Dark clouds swallowed the cranes. The aviation beacons

were muffled, as if they shone from inside the belly of a great beast. Nevan's crane was locked, standing side-on, getting walloped by the wind. Jack could only imagine how horrible it must be in there considering he could barely keep his feet on the ground. *Idiot.* Though he could not admonish him too much, Nevan was a few years younger and had a polish to his enthusiasm that had long worn off Jack's. To him, the job was just the job, until a better one came along. The higher-ups made you feel like you should almost live in the cab. *Surely they're not having him do lifts in this.*

The streets were practically empty because of the storm. Late-night fancy bars and restaurants had only a few staff members inside. He felt their eyes on him, as if they knew this was not his part of town. It often struck him that he was helping to build a city that he would never be able to afford to live in.

There was no doorman on duty, which suited Jack. He went straight to the elevator and found the apartment in the maze of identical doors. No Christmas decorations adorned Ronan's temporary home – minimalist in style and completely lacking any personal touch. Ronan's suitcases still stood by the door, like he was in a constant state of readiness to leave. Large glass windows overlooked the city and river. *What's the point in them giving you this, when they don't give you the time to enjoy it?*

The fridge was full of frozen dinners. He stuck one in the microwave, showered quickly and changed into his spare clothes. He sat in front of the telly with a beer and felt all cheer vanish when he realised it was non-alcoholic. The rain fell so heavily now that he could hear it drumming against the thick, noise-cancelling windows. *No work tomorrow.*

"Breaking news…" The voices on the television became distant as he started nodding off. He turned the film off, having no interest in what he thought was the start of a post-apocalyptic horror. He went to bed and was asleep before the blankets warmed up.

10

TOWER CRANE

The phone vibrated across the bedside locker, luring Jack from a vanishing dream. When it stopped, he nearly fell back to sleep before it rang again. Drool crusted the side of his face. He could barely open his eyes. Disorientation at waking in a strange place vanished with the worry of seeing so many missed calls.

"What? Ronan, what's the matter?"

"Nevan's not responding. He's still in the crane."

Jack got out of bed and ran straight for the living room. It was still dark out. The storm had only worsened. Looking through the window was like trying to peer through a bottle of ink. "Have you been out of touch with him long?"

"Since before you left."

"The radio's probably busted. You know yourself, every week he makes a report about faulty wiring, but nothing's ever done. He's stuck up there now until this weather clears."

"That's fair enough, but he's not let the lock off for the wind. The crane's stuck in place. It won't stand the storm."

Jack caught himself before reacting. He did not want to fuel Ronan's worry.

"You wouldn't be able to go up after him would you?"

"You're right Ronan, I wouldn't. Not in this. What could I do if I did? It would take me an hour to reach him and I wouldn't be able to bring him back down. Only difference would be that the two of us would be stuck up there. Stop worrying. He knows what he's doing. I was chatting to him over the phone earlier. He's okay. He's as good on the controls as I am. He's probably riding out the wind as best he sees fit from up there."

"So long as the crane doesn't come down on the city."

"You worrying is not going to solve the problem. Would you get to bed, I feel like your wife. I doubt we'll be lifting much tomorrow and that's not on you."

"When the wind dies down we'll have to. I've been on the phone all night. Got some replacement drivers to deliver the cement. Sorry for waking you, go back to bed. I'll be there in an hour or so. Just wanted to get your opinion."

"Do you know what it probably is? He takes these deadly videos and pictures of the city. He has a great camera for it. Might just be staying up there to get footage for his Instagram account."

"Yeah, maybe." Ronan did not sound convinced.

Jack returned to the spare room and covered himself with the thick blanket. *That eejit is in for a horrible night.*

There was an undercurrent of sirens wailing just below the storm.

* * *

Jack tossed and turned for the rest of the night. The call played on his mind until he fumbled in the dark to turn off his alarm. He rubbed sleep from his eyes and got up. *This is no way to live.* If not for the fact that he had bills to pay, he would have considered pulling a sickie.

Trying not to wake Ronan, he sneaked through the kitchen. The rain seemed to have calmed a little. He turned the television on while preparing breakfast.

"A state of emergency has been declared."

He changed the channel, trying to find the news. It acted as background noise to keep him awake.

Commotion in the hall outside the apartment was louder than the noise of the coffee machine. Jack washed his thermos and stuck it beneath the spout. Then he went to the peephole to investigate. People rushed past the door. *Living in the heart of Dublin, you'd imagine you could have a lie-on.*

"...chaos in Dublin." Jack turned to look at the television. The footage showed hospitals completely overrun with patients. *Oh my heart.* After the conversation with Ronan, he half-expected to see the wreckage of a fallen crane scarring the city. *I should get a flu shot.* He turned the television off and went to shower.

* * *

When he closed the door to the apartment, the queue of people waiting by the elevator turned and stared at him with a mixture of fear and apprehension. Some wore bulging backpacks, while others pulled heavy suitcases behind them. *When was the last time I went on a holiday?* Apartment doors opened as residents in dressing gowns and pajamas stepped out to see what all the fuss was about. When the elevator door opened people tried to rush in, but there was no space left.

"Is it a joke?" somebody asked.

Jack heard crying coming from an apartment down the hall. His anxiety peaked as he followed people heading for the emergency stairs. Anybody he asked for information just shrugged or ignored him. Those behind started pushing, trying to get out. It was like an alarm was ringing and he was the only one who could not hear it.

Panic was infectious. People covered their mouths with sleeves or dishcloths. *Gas? Fire?* The lobby was crowded. The front doors were shuttered. People outside were trying to get in, while those inside could not get out.

Jack followed the signs for the underground car park. Engines revved and horns blared as people tried to drive out. Twice he was nearly knocked over.

It couldn't be a dream, not with the pain from others treading on his feet and knocking into him. Nobody knew what was happening. None of the cars on the ramp to the main road were moving. Jack left through a fire exit. The alarm rang in the underground, but it did not upset people anymore than they already were. Only when he reached the street above could he hear the chaos that was engulfing the capital.

The roads were clogged and impassable. A horn blared behind him, and he turned just in time to see a car mount the kerb. Jack threw himself backwards. The car sped by him, running over a woman who was not quick enough to dodge it. The driver didn't slow down. Jack tried to catch the registration plate; it was a brand new car, but the driver had used it like a battering ram.

The woman was still conscious. Jack picked himself up, his only damage was shock and grazed palms. Adrenaline kept him numb to pain. "Are you okay?" he asked.

The woman tried to crawl away from him on her elbows. She winced, grimaced and screamed.

A Ring of Oak & Apple

"Calm down. That maniac's gone. Are you okay?"

Jack looked up just as the driver crashed into stalled traffic on the main road. It was only then that he noticed that the cars ahead were empty. *People are abandoning their vehicles.* Those behind had no idea they were beeping at nobody.

"Get away from me," the woman said.

"I'm trying to help. Here, don't get up, you might have broken something. I'll call an ambulance."

She turned pale. "Please don't. Just leave me alone."

Jack did not listen to her protests. He called for help, trying to catch the eye of people running by, but onlookers ignored him. When he rang the emergency services, it went straight to a recording. "Leave your address and number after the tone. Remain indoors. Do not engage the infected. Stay away from hospitals and built up areas."

The woman dragged herself to the side of the building to rest against it. "Just leave me alone, I'll be okay in a minute."

"Are you sure?"

She roared at him and, despite his better judgement, he left. Jack stopped asking people what happened after several shouted at him to piss off. One man was about to take a swing at him for getting too close. The background noise of the city had become strange, like there was a football match going on and the home team was losing. Where one cluster of people ran away from, others hurried towards. The only safe place he could think to go to was the building site, with its high, sturdy fences.

"Epidemic." "Fatalities." "Emergency services unable to cope." "Stay indoors." He was able to piece some information together from cars with their radios on. None of it made much sense. He nearly collided with a man in a suit. He had been trying to ask for information. Jack was the only person to stop long enough to speak with him.

"My phone isn't working," the man said.

"Turn around and go home. Get out of the city. I don't know what's happening."

"War? Nuclear power plant accident at Sellafield? Asteroid? Where are you heading?"

"To my car," Jack said.

"You won't drive out of here. The city's backed up."

"Well then – I don't know."

"Good luck," the man said, before melting into the scared mass of people.

Why did he have to go and say a thing like 'good luck'? If it's an asteroid, then nothing on the building site will help. Even with that thought, Jack made a note to go straight to the rack of hard helmets.

The site was locked and the usual security guard was absent. Jack fumbled with his keycard and pressed it against the pad for the rotating gate. He said a silent prayer, but abandoned it as soon as the gate unlocked. Lights were shining from the office. Ronan was inside, glued to a small television screen. He let out a roar when Jack entered.

"Thank fuck." Jack found it hard to catch his breath. "What's happening?"

Ronan just looked at Jack and made to speak, but no words came out. On screen, satellite images of Dublin were superimposed with a red border. The title read 'Quarantine Zone'. Instructions on how to avoid infection ran across the bottom of the screen. Footage from inside a hospital showed people acting strange and weeping. Patients were restrained.

Before Jack knew what was happening, his legs went from under him. He fell flat on the ground. Ronan turned in the swivel chair. Dublin was dying and they were trapped in the middle of it.

The spell was broken by the sound of screeching metal. It made every hair on Jack's body stand on end. "That's a crane. Did Nevan come down?"

"No," Ronan said. His panic turned to terror.

Jack had never heard it before, but he knew it was the sound of a dying crane.

11

THE TOWER FELL

The screams and cries of terrified people paled in comparison to the metallic groans of the crane.

"Ronan, get him on the phone now," Jack said.

"I've been trying for hours. He's not answering."

"Is that crane going to fall?"

The breath left Ronan and he nodded. "Yes."

"No – like, it's not going to fall in the next few minutes?"

Ronan shrugged. "I hope not."

"You're a great man for building confidence. If I take the lock off, will that be enough?"

"I don't know!"

Jack put on a hard hat, hi-vis jacket and gloves. The wind was still daunting, but he had little choice. "Is there anybody on his site?"

Ronan looked at him as if the conversation had just registered. "You can't go up there you daft bastard. You won't come down – or you will, but much quicker than's good for you."

"What happens if that falls?"

Ronan's mouth hung open for a while before he spoke.

"It could lodge against one of the buildings. Harmlessly." But Jack could see by his expression that that outcome would be miraculous.

"Even if it doesn't land on anybody, if it blocks the road... people will die. Focus. Can you reach anybody on the site?"

"No. You'll have to go over the wall."

Each time the grating of the crane ceased, Jack's hope swelled that he would not hear it again. Ronan looked on the verge of shock. Beneath his body-warmer was a considerable paunch. *Can't ask him to do it.* "Do something to make the site safer while I'm gone." He wanted to keep the man's mind occupied. "Park a few trucks in front of the gates." Even saying it sounded stupid, but Ronan nodded. Jack looked at his car and wished he could be outside the city limits, heading for his home in rural Ireland. *One job and then I'm gone.*

Jack walked through the metal turnstile onto the street. It felt like being an extra on the set of a movie and he was waiting for the director to yell cut. *Any minute now.* He could barely spare his attention from the madness on street level to look up, but every time he did, he flinched, expecting to be swallowed by the crane's looming shadow.

Buses were full of confused passengers. People stood by their cars, unsure about leaving them. The rapid burst of what could only be gunfire made everybody slow. *Can this actually be happening?* After that, people tried to get inside the office buildings and hotels just off the road. *This can't be a dream. If I ever saw those horrified faces in sleep, I'd never close my eyes.*

It felt unnatural to sprint through the streets of Dublin. His lungs burned and he cursed himself for letting his casual smoking habit become an addiction. He slowed for a teenager blocking the path, he was distraught and weeping.

He kept turning on the spot, as if looking for somebody amidst the confusion. When he set eyes on Jack, he lunged. Somebody shouldered Jack out of the way and struck the teen a vicious blow to the head with a hurling stick. The attacker snarled and struck him a few more times, ensuring the teen would never rise again.

"What are you doing? Stop!" The words caught in Jack's throat when the man turned on him.

Anguish painted his face. "Why? Was he not weeping? Oh – no."

"He was."

The man looked relieved enough to cry. "If you see anybody weeping, you run away. They're infected."

"You're crying," Jack said.

The man hesitated before putting a hand to his face. It came away wet with tears and blood.

Loud screeching echoed above them. "I need to get to the building site down the road," Jack said. "There's a tower crane going to fall and if that blocks the road, there'll be no getting out of Dublin through the Port Tunnel."

The man laughed. "Some string of bad luck today, eh? Come on then."

The sheer scale of the madness was breathtaking. Dodging refugees while wondering what they were seeking refuge from. Running side by side with a murderer.

The gates to the site were locked and nobody answered his calls. When his keycard failed, he tried kicking at the boards in the wall out of desperation, but the shock only travelled right back up his leg. "Boost me up..."

"Call me Kevin. Alright, come on. Toss over a ladder when you're on the other side." Kevin squatted with his back against the wall and knotted his fingers together. "Don't leave me hanging."

A Ring of Oak & Apple

Jack ground the bottom of his boot against the path to clean it, then stood in Kevins' hands. He boosted him high enough to grab the edge of the wall and he pulled himself over. The site was empty, but it was only when Jack was half-dangling over the other side that he wondered if any of the crazies had gotten in. *I just watched a man die.*

He landed hard. The site had a revolving door that worked freely so long as you were leaving. He wasted valuable time searching for a ladder. When he found one, he placed it against the wall and climbed up. "Sorry it took so long, Kevin. Nearly there."

When he got to the top, Kevin was nowhere in sight. Jack pulled the ladder up, balanced it on the top of the wall and let it fall onto the street. He lowered himself back into the site. *Somebody can use it.*

Acid rose in his throat the closer he came to the base of the crane. He rested his forehead on the cool metal of a ladder rung and vomited before starting the climb.

Above the protection of the walls the wind howled through the metal mesh cage. When he looked out over the city, the unnatural sight took away his fear of heights. He was almost glad to be above the horrors below. The water of the river churned from the sheer number of people swimming in it. Windows that would normally have been dark at this hour were lit up with watching silhouettes. Jack's hand missed a rung. There was only a brief moment of emptiness before his fingers hit it. The damage to the crane was extensive.

Go back. Could I live with myself if this fell and I did nothing? He kept climbing, rising now at a slight angle.

When he reached the top, he pulled himself onto the platform and crawled to the cab on his belly.

Nevan was still in his chair. Worry turned to rage. Jack

punched the window with the side of his fist. "What the hell are you playing at? Take the lock off!"

Nevan started and moved towards the noise. His head bounced off the glass. Jack did not hear the weeping until the door was open, until it was too late. Nevan's expression never changed. His face was slate grey and the whites of his bloodshot eyes were a jaundiced yellow. His jaw shivered up and down, modulating the sound of his weeping. He struggled to draw breath.

Jack reacted out of panic. For the second time that morning, he blindly fell backwards out of danger. His heart did not start beating until he felt the railing against his back. He slammed the door, but it caught against Nevan's arm and did not close.

Nevan tripped out of the cab and landed on the platform between Jack and the ladder. Jack prepared to jump over him and try to descend, but stopped. *I can't leave. Especially if it means turning my back to him.*

"Cop on, Nev!"

Nevan tried to stand, but he could barely carry himself. His hands were ruined and bloody. He leaned on his left arm awkwardly and fell face first after a sickening crack announced his wrist had snapped.

Jack walked onto the gimbal. The wind snapped at his clothes. When it died down, his own efforts to keep his balance nearly caused him to fall off the other edge. "Stop! Please."

Nevan crawled after him like he was senselessly drunk. He gained his feet, stumbled in his haste and fell off the crane. He did not call out or scream. Jack dropped down and grabbed the gangway. He watched his friend plummet, pick up speed, his clothes fluttering. The sound of his impact

A Ring of Oak & Apple

barely registered against the noise of fear and death outside the site.

Jack's muscles seized. "No, no, no." He held onto the crane with an iron grip. He did not think he would ever be able to let go, until the crane shuddered from a strong gust and he was sure it would fall. He dragged himself towards the platform, inch by inch. Every buffet of wind made him cry out.

He covered his mouth before opening the door to the cab. Holding his breath, he took the lock off the crane, hoping it was not too late. Hugging the railing, he started the descent. From the noise of the city, he expected to see pillars of smoke and fire raging across the capital, but it was a city of stone, glass and metal. Only the people would break.

I'm shaking. He realised with dread that he was not. The crane was moving. He slipped, reached out blindly and caught his arm awkwardly in the ladder. There was a snap, followed by instant nausea and incredible pain. The crane cried out too. He reached back for the ladder, cradling the injured arm to his chest.

Too high up. He could not get the image of Nevan falling out of his mind. Despite holding on, he was still falling. With everything to gain, he went as fast as he could. His left shoulder throbbed and his ribs hurt so much that every breath was excruciating. The stars in his vision threatened to blind him.

When he reached the ground, he ran as fast as he could away from the crane. He vomited, letting the bile cover his front. He did not make it far before the light dimmed and the crane's shadow grew.

12

ESCAPE

"I remember that," Eilish said. "They showed the footage so often on the news that it became the symbol for the fall of Dublin. I thought it was done on purpose to stop people spreading the disease. What was it like?"

Jack flexed his shoulder and winced. "To watch it fall? Horrifying. You can't really get a feel for how large these things are until you're sitting on top of one, or standing right beneath it as it's coming down. Try looking up the side of a skyscraper. A couple of tonnes of towering steel, rending itself apart. Maybe had I left it locked, it would have held a little longer. It scraped across the bones of the building site next to it. If there was any luck left in the world, it would have stuck there, but it slid off and toppled onto the street, cutting off escape through the Port Tunnel."

Fin held out his bottle and clinked it off Jack's. "Here's to trying. You know, they sent drones into the tunnel, the crane toppling probably saved a few lives if it kept people out of there. Anybody you kept off ships and ferries at Dublin Port certainly lived longer on land than they did in the Irish Sea."

"Yeah, but at least they got to experience a bit of hope before they died. I forget what that feels like," Jack said.

"What did you do then?" Eilish asked.

"I went back to my site. Ronan let people in while I was gone. We didn't know what the hell to do, or what to look out for. With the city in the state it was, the only safe place to go was up. Longest climb of my life. Ronan brought enough food and water to keep us a while. Thought we were going to die in my crane. Surely the military would have fixed everything in a matter of hours. Days went by and mostly the only noticeable change was there was less screaming and more weeping. You could feel the trembling of the city through the crane. The sound of explosions and gunfire was weird. What was worse though was their absence. After a while, there was only the sounds of nature. The city wept. I was on so many painkillers that I'm not sure what was a dream and what was reality."

"What happened to Ronan?" Eilish asked.

"Same thing that happened to most of the country. I couldn't do much with my arm, but I used the crane to help other survivors in surrounding buildings and they helped us. Even after the power went, we were hooked up to a navy vessel on the Liffey."

"I have to go to the bathroom." Josh spoke for the first time since the incident with Fin. He rocked on his haunches. Fin noticed how antsy he had become over the course of Jack's story.

"Nobody's going to hold it for you," Eilish said. "Just don't piss near the tents."

Josh jumped to his feet. "Can I have a cigarette, please?"

The people here were more forgiving than Fin first thought. They clearly felt for the man and must have imagined that he could fit in, given time. Somebody took out a cigarette and a lighter and tossed them to him. Josh disappeared into the underbrush without a word of thanks.

"What are we supposed to do with him?" Jack asked. "I mean, we're picking up new people every day. There's enough food for all of us and more than enough work. But I don't feel comfortable around him."

"Maybe he just overreacted," Eilish said in a whisper. "To be fair, we did just kill his friend. Having to listen to grim camp stories over a fire with the strangers who killed somebody close to him, I don't think I'd be calm."

"It's mad isn't it?" Fin said. "Had things continued as normal a few weeks ago, we'd all have gone our entire lives without ever meeting. We could have walked a foot apart and never known. Before this happened, I would have imagined that lad would have been a boy racer, or at worst, he littered. Now though we've no way of reading people, of knowing how far they'll go. This has messed with all of our heads."

"You're one to talk," Eilish said. "You've a knife the size of a sabre, a concealed pistol and a rifle that looks like it could leave a dent in the moon. From all of that, I would have guessed you were a crazy prepper living in the attic of a Tesco's. Hoarding and waiting."

Fin smiled. "I wish. I'm not staying, so I don't have a say in it. Though if I was, I wouldn't force him out. Maybe he just needs time to settle. Watch him and keep him busy. I don't think he has the stomach for killing."

"Not directly," Jack said. "He just has the mouth for it."

"Certainly not the trousers," Eilish scoffed.

"I probably went too far," Fin said. "Hurt pride is a hard thing to overcome. There's no probably about it, I did go too far. I've often wet myself since this started. Nearly curried my trousers a few times, too."

Jack scoffed at the term. "We can't convince you to stay?"

Fin shook his head.

"You'll not find better where you're heading," Jack said. "This is the first place where I can sleep through the nightmares, without fear of being torn apart while my eyes are closed. There's nothing for me at home. If I even make it that far. I lost hope and that'll keep me alive. You'd be wise to rid yourself of it too."

"Oh trust me, I have," Fin said. "Whole country is untethered. Holding on to 'home' will get you killed. Rich, I know, coming from the man crossing the country to get there."

Jack shook his head. "Only thing you can hope for out east is a quick death. Quick and relatively painless."

"Only reason I'm here now is because others died instead of me," Fin said. "I don't believe in ghosts, but I believe in guilt and I can't settle just yet with that haunting me. This isn't a bad place you have here..."

Something fizzed in the woods making them all go quiet. Before they could pinpoint the sound it vanished leaving a terrible and brief silence. A deafening shriek shattered it. A white, blinding light shot into the sky on a pillar of smoke and fire. The firework screamed as it rose and erupted with an explosion above the island, illuminating the valley for a moment.

The calm that had come over them through easy conversations and drink was destroyed. All of them were up with weapons drawn. The smell of gunpowder from the rocket scented the air.

"That prick," Jack cursed. "The dead from horizon to horizon will have heard that."

They listened. Fin was almost hopeful, until the sound

of distant weeping carried across the lake from every direction.

Ian rushed through the undergrowth, scanned the fearful expressions of those in the camp, and hurried on towards the site of the firework.

Fin ran after him. "Some of you stay here. Make sure Josh doesn't come back to take anything." He gripped the handle of his hammer. This was as close as he had ever come to looking forward to using it on the living.

He ran along the narrow path without waiting to see who followed. Branches scratched at his face. Brambles and briars tripped his feet. Immediately after leaving behind the fire, Fin was forced to slow down – it would be an easy thing to twist an ankle on the uneven ground. *He could be waiting behind any tree with a rock, ready to cave my skull in.* That thought slowed him further, he did not want to end his days on this island. *Those behind might mistake me for Josh and attack first out of fear. Chaos.*

Fin reached the shore without encountering anybody. Ian stood just above the waterline. He panted, either from the run or sheer anger. "He's in the lake."

"Does he have a boat?" Eilish asked.

Fin followed the sound. It did not take long for his eyes to adjust in the moonlight. Josh struggled far from the shore. From the sound of it, he could barely breathe with his shivering. With each desperate stroke of his arm unsettling the water, Josh drew more attention from the opposite shores. Fin could see silhouettes massing, riled in anticipation.

"You'll freeze to death before you reach the shore, you idiot," Eilish said.

By the light of the full moon, Fin watched his frantic

thrashing. Josh yelped, haunted by the monsters he thought were chasing him from the island.

"Come back!" The anger in Fin's voice caught him by surprise. If he were at the receiving end of it, it would only serve to hasten his retreat. In a similar situation he might have done the same thing, but setting off a firework was suicide and likely would cause the deaths of more than just him.

"Quiet." Ian knelt down. His voice lowered to a whisper. "Get back to the tree cover. Spread the word to be silent. Put that fire out."

A crowd of monsters gathered by the old dockyard. At first, Fin thought he was listening to the wind, but he realised it was the horde of undead rushing through the woods and fields towards them. Josh begged for help while choking on lake water.

The noise of the infected drew more undead. It was a domino effect; once you brought enough attention to yourself, weepers would be attracted by the sound of other weepers.

Suddenly the lake between them felt like only a puddle. The reeds whispered. Water gurgled over mud and stone. The exhausted, exasperated gasps of Josh became distant. His splashing slowed, but not, Fin thought, out of awareness of the weepers. *He'll be dead soon. If he survives, he might draw them off, though.*

"Come back," Fin said, despite his anger. The thought of that man out there between assumed killers and the weepers did not sit well with him. To drown in freezing water. His body would drift away from the moonlight to be swallowed by centuries of silt on the lakebed, without leaving a letter to those he loved.

Mist hovered above the lake. Fin cupped his shaking

hands in front of his mouth and blew heat into them. In this weather, he would exhaust his lungs before they warmed. "Where are they all coming from? My map showed a small town nearby and a cluster of villages. There's too much empty space for this many."

"There's a national road that bypasses the town," Jack said. "We saw a lot of them there, but not this many. Something's riled them."

The rivers here were slow moving and went through the hearts of large towns. Fin knew he could not survive them with so many infected around. "Do you have enough food on the island?"

"Why?" Eilish asked.

"Because we might be stuck here for a while," Fin said. He shuddered at the thought of what was going on in the surrounding woods. Weepers rushing through the dark, squealing their anguished cries. *How many will get caught in briars or run straight into the lake? Not nearly enough.*

"We just wait it out and be quiet, then?" Eilish asked.

"I don't think it's that easy," Ian said. "The weepers on the shore are going to cause the weepers further away to start crying, they'll bring more and more. Imagine an avalanche of teeth and clawing fingers. That rocket just turned them all towards us."

"Look at them," Jack said. "For every weeper isn't there supposed to be two zombies?"

"I think it's closer to four now," Eilish said. "Should we go after Josh?" Her teeth chattered. "He's going to die if we don't."

"No," Fin said. "He's going to die because of what he did. If he returned, we'd only have to kill him. Besides, we'd only draw more attention. What if he screams for us to get away?

A Ring of Oak & Apple

If he's willing to fire a rocket, then let him leave. He'd only be a liability here."

Fin went back with the others to the fire. He savoured the last bit of heat with a heavy heart, before they doused it. The weeping echoed louder in the darkness.

Ian spoke first. "Party's over, I'm afraid. That rocket will draw every weeper in the valley. We'll have to start a watch. It's not long until morning. We'll break up into groups and patrol the shoreline."

"But the dead can't swim," a young woman said, almost petulantly. "We're on an island."

"Weepers in the water won't survive, but they'll become zombies and they could wash up. There are that many that the wind will favour some and blow them out to us. If you're too drunk to be of any use, then sleep it off. You'll take the day watch."

"We could be lucky," Jack said. "The sound will have travelled around the hills. Not even survivors could accurately pinpoint our location. We just need to be quiet and keep hidden for a few days until they lose interest."

"Where did he get the rocket? Does he have more of them?" somebody asked.

"He took it from my kayak," Fin said. "I was worried he took something personal, so I never noticed one of the rockets was missing. I doubt he could survive the swim in this temperature. If he does, a rocket surely won't."

"You shouldn't have scared him like that," somebody said.

Fin opened his mouth to argue, but he could not defend his actions. "I know. I'm as scared as all of you. I thought it better to bark instead of bite." *That man – no, that boy – is going to die hating me.*

"Fin didn't light the fuse. Keep noise to a minimum. Let's start our watch," Ian said. "We can come up with a plan in the morning. Maybe the infected will have wandered off by then."

Somebody picked up a bucket of water and poured it over the last dying embers of the fire. They hissed and went out, leaving them with only the light of the curious moon. In the darkness they lost their humanity, became indistinguishable from the infected. Fin grasped the hammer, trying to still his quickening heart. *They're not sick.*

Fin followed Ian back to the lake's edge. By now the natural world was silent. There was too much weeping to hear anything else.

13

GOODBYE

The moon shrivelled and dwindled away before the first hint of morning tinged the horizon. The birds had fled their roosts during the night, spooked by the sound of the undead. Fin doubted they would return.

With the help of Ian, he carried his kayak to the shore. They used it as a windbreaker. His hot water bottle had long gone cold.

"So what's your story?" Ian asked. His breath misted in the air.

Fin buried his hands under his armpits. The chill was a constant corrosive. "Not much different to yours, I'd imagine." He was not in the mood to reminisce about a world that no longer existed.

There was enough light in the day for them to see the extent of the weeper infestation. The hills writhed with their bodies. They attacked their own kind with indifference. *Not even animals act in such a way.*

"I heard you talking earlier about intelligent infected," Ian said. "I can't say looking at them now that I can imagine it. Maybe they'll wipe themselves out."

"I hope they do because I don't think we can. How have you survived all this time?" Fin opened a tube of effervescent vitamin tablets and gave one to Ian. He popped two in his water bottle and listened to them fizz.

"Like you said, there aren't any innocent survivors. Not anymore."

Fin had a dull headache from the alcohol. He wished he could go a night without it, but it took the edge off. "Struggling over morality seems like something you waste time on when there's peace. Right now, there are the desperate and the dead. You're either one or the other. There's no room for anything else."

"I like that line of thinking, for now," Ian said. "I'm just worried about the toll that'll be due when this ends."

"You're worried about something that might never happen. It's optimistic to think that there'll be an end to this. Enough of that talk anyway. It's best had in front of a fire, on the better side of drunk. How are you set here for food?"

"Well," Ian said, "I had plans to try and catch some of the crows. Take from that what you will. There are enough farms around here with grain and seed stores. Sheds of potatoes, too. If they kept, we'd be grand. But they'll go off before too long."

"Crows are clever. They might not return if you do that. Meat might be infected too if they're eating the dead, which they undoubtedly are."

Across the water, some of the isolated weepers stood still like dark monoliths, ignorant to the cold, waiting for stimulation.

"You mentioned you thought some followed you," Ian said.

Even now Fin was uncertain. "Eilish put my mind to rest.

A Ring of Oak & Apple

Every large town had the same chain of clothing stores. Let's just say, I've seen some acting strange. Anyway. I might have a solution to your crowd problem. I've to keep moving. I'll pass on down the river. I have a few more fireworks. It'll take some attention off the island."

"Remember when we first met and I said you wouldn't be thought poorly of for forgetting to bring a bottle of wine? Well we'd appreciate the wine a lot more than you killing yourself on our account. Besides, the wind's against you. It'll be a hard slog out in the open. With the sun rising, you'll be the only target on the lake."

It did not take Fin long to weigh up his options. There was only one choice, really. Solene and his family needed him. *Maybe we could come back here. I have to keep moving before it's too late.* Too much had already been lost to this cause. "There's not enough drink on this island for me to drown out the ghosts of my sins." His was a pilgrimage of sorts. A penance was owed. "I'll leave and draw them off and lose them on the river."

Ian blew out a breath. "Suppose fences and hedges will net them for the most part."

"It's not bad here at all," Fin said. "A little bit of paradise, or it will be, in summer. You only have to block off the infected. The rest is farmland. Easily defensible. Maybe start planting in spring and wait for the salmon to come back up the river."

"It'll be a long time before anybody feels comfortable taking anything from the river. You do make it sound appealing though. Why not stay, rest even? I've a few hours left in me to stand watch."

"Thank you, but I've a long while yet to go before I can rest." Fin considered it for a moment before handing the man his rifle. He gave him the two full clips from the kayak as well. "I can't exactly practice without drawing weepers. Besides, I don't think there's enough ammunition for me to better my aim."

Ian tested the weight of it. "What makes you think I'd be any better with it?"

"It's not for the infected. Remember, there are no innocent survivors. I've had more trouble with the living than the dead lately."

"When you get where you're going, if you find nothing there, you're needed here."

"If I had nowhere else to be, I'd stay. Boat out a few portable sheds and building materials. Wouldn't be warm to start, but it'd be safe enough."

"In general you speak like you trust nobody, but you're after giving me a rifle."

"I haven't given you the firing pin yet," Fin said.

* * *

They laboured over maps for a while. Ian had people come and add notes about the obstacles ahead. There were larger lakes to come. That was where he planned to lose the horde. The trail behind him was riddled with his own notes and references. A few people looked at them and walked away poorer for the knowledge.

The sheer number of infected convinced many of the survivors that the island was the best possible place to be. If they did not think Fin was mad for his interactions with Josh, then their suspicions were confirmed when he committed to leaving.

As much as Fin said he had foregone hope, he had harboured a little that he would make it home. Looking at

A Ring of Oak & Apple

the fresh ink covering the map, indicating the horrors to come, Fin's last ember of hope was extinguished. Ireland had become a no man's land, filled with dead towns and ravenous weepers. Love letters to the lost. *How did these people make it out?*

When the crowd gathered around the map thinned, a man approached. Fin had not heard him speak during the night. He kept to himself and had that horrible stare Fin associated with a tormented mind. He scanned the page. "I'm heading back to Mayo. Any suggestions?"

"Don't. You'll find nothing there except ash and death. If I knew it would make a difference, I'd beg you not to go."

The man took his hands from his pockets and started absent-mindedly twisting the wedding band on his finger. Fin passed a lot of people that were on similar pilgrimages to him. Some just wanted to die where they belonged, wandering bones seeking their final resting place. If they could put family members, neighbours and friends to rest as well, then all the better.

He matched Fin's stare. "I'll bury them in ash then."

"Bury them deep." He recounted his journey to the man, giving him his best estimates on where he could find food.

Fin returned to the ringfort for his last meal. He sat and listened to the islanders discussing what they were going to do next. He felt separate from their troubles, though he could empathise. There was enough light to chance a cooking fire and a large pot of stew was already bubbling above the flames. Fin put a small pot of water on to boil for his hot water bottle.

"Trust me when I say we're not in a bad position here," Eilish said. "The hills around will have muffled the sound and kept most of the weepers away. It's cold and miserable out here, but the water protects us."

Fin grimaced at the memory of an island off the coast of Westport, at how he had thought getting there would solve all his problems. His mind went to the whiskey at the recollection, but they were all empty. *I'll have to find more before the day's out.* During his darkest moments, he could hear the echo of a memory, the sound a hammer makes against a human skull.

"Don't become complacent," Ian said. "We were lucky last night, but those things will wash up on the shore, eventually. We only drink water from the catchment barrels. If you bathe, you're better off doing it in an inch of water. Nobody wants to be the horror movie gobshite that dies because of stupidity. I don't know if you heard what happened on the Aran Islands? We're standing on a pebble in comparison to them."

There were a few sombre nods at that. Fin pored over the map, trying to memorise different routes. Though he knew when it came down to running for his life, street names just seemed to slip his mind. Some of the younger people busied themselves cleaning the firepit and laying new wood for the coming night. The ring of stones around the pit was built higher.

I want to stay. He took the perfume from his pocket and held the cap beneath his nose. That was all the constitution he needed. He listened to them talking about nearby stables, post office supply depots and farms they found while scouting. The voices melted together as drowsiness overcame him. It was the perfume, her smell was too much of a comfort.

"Find fences, we can make this a proper fort."

"Fields close to the shore look fit for farming. Could be something to consider in the spring."

"There are some stocked lakes around here, we could try

to find them, see if they're clear of infection. Would be worth it for the meat."

Fin closed his eyes as the heat from the cookfire worked its way through his clothes. When he tried to open them again, the lids felt like they were weighted. Every waking moment he craved the blissful oblivion of sleep, though these days the terror often followed him into his dreams. He had little choice but to let darkness consume him.

* * *

He was back on the water, watching the man about to enter the river. He had time to call out, to try and stop him, but he stayed silent, choosing to fight the current of conscience that was sweeping him towards the man. When the man went under, Fin felt relieved. It was no longer his responsibility to help. He paddled to the location and looked for the body. The water was clear as glass. The man was caught in roots on the riverbed. He stared right up at Fin.

"I'm sorry." He knew the man could not hear him and even if he could, it was not enough. "Sleep softly and dream of nothing." His whole body shivered as he remembered saying that to those in need, those desperately helpless. Those that he could only offer mercy to in the form of a quick and painless death.

There were other faces half-buried in the silt, all familiar. They looked calm and welcoming, but there was nothing serene about their expressions; marbled, like statues on a gallows. There was Josh. No longer scared or angry. Fin was not sure if some of them were waving for him to join, or if the current had just taken control of their lifeless limbs. He could no longer breathe, but he fought the urge to enter the water. Until he saw Solene's pale face.

Without a second thought, he dove in. After the burst of bubbles all he heard was weeping.

He woke, gasping for air, drenched in a cold sweat.

The camp had changed considerably over the several hours he had slept through. The ever-present weeping had subsided.

People stopped, startled by his panic, but soon returned to their chores. Some washed clothing in basins, while others were putting up wooden fences outside the ringfort. A few were digging trenches. "How did I sleep through that?"

"By the look of it, your body had two options," Eilish said. "Sleep or die. I thought you'd died."

Fin sat up and rubbed his face. The action got some disapproving looks from people he had not once seen without masks and gloves on.

"There's coffee in the pot," somebody said. "No milk, though."

Fin took a mug gratefully. The old stone of the ringfort, covered in moss and old leaves, was a comfort from the wind. It created a little bowl of heat when the sun shone.

"You know, if you stayed, you'd be a real help to us," Ian said as he sat down beside him.

Fin already felt a strong affinity towards them. The only reason he was bothered by Ian asking was because he wanted nothing more than to stay. *Just one more night, Solene.* He tried desperately to fix the memory of her face in his mind. "I want to, but I can't. I wish you all the luck in the world".

Eilish lifted her grubby lottery ticket at that. "Already told you, we don't need luck."

Fin smiled. "Once this is over, I'll find you. When you cash in your millions we'll be the best of friends."

"It'll cost you your story," Eilish said.

"It's not much different to any of yours." The coffee was dark and rich, evoking a wealth of painful memories. "My world ended the last time I saw Solene, I just didn't know it at the time."

READ FINS STORY IN WEEP BOOK ONE: THE IRISH EPIDEMIC

PICK UP YOUR COPY HERE
www.eoinbradybooks.com

There is no evacuation.
Survival will cost your humanity.
Expected death toll: a nation.
Yesterday Fin was a nightporter. Today he is a survivor.

WEEP 1 THE IRISH EPIDEMIC

Within days the outbreak devoured Ireland. It started with a fever hot enough to burn away the soul. What remained was violent, deranged and ravenous, no longer human: weepers. At first, they lured victims with anguished cries. Now, the sound causes terror. The sick must hunt.

Death offers no rest from the disease and the infected rise again to spread the plague as **zombies.**

Fearing pandemic, foreign warships quarantine Ireland, seeking containment at all cost. Chaos and panic engulf a world preparing for the end. While at home, a dwindling population flee ruined cities, forced into a frozen countryside of vacant graves.

Extinction has been stopped - for now.

In what could be the last days of recorded history, Fin must survive amongst the desperate and the dead to find his family - on the opposite side of Ireland, no matter the cost.

How much of yourself would you give to save the ones you love?

WEEP 2 SLACK JAW

There are no innocent survivors in an Ireland overrun with weepers.

Commercial skipper Samantha Prendergast has an engagement ring in her pocket and a question on her mind as she sails across a stormy Atlantic Ocean. She only has hours to ask it before the Weeping Plague destroys a nation.

Nothing about The Irish Epidemic seemed natural and now Samantha can prove it. When she uncovers a secret that could save the human race and a conspiracy to cover it up, she has no choice but to take action. It could be her only hope of finding a cure for her infected loved ones.

ABOUT THE AUTHOR

Eoin Brady is the author of post-apocalyptic horror, epic fantasy and contemporary romance novels. Most are set in Ireland, where he lives and writes. Weep, his most recent story, begins on the west coast of Ireland, as the country is ravaged by a horrifying disease.

Keep up to date on new books releasing at www.eoinbradybooks.com

Copyright

Copyright © 2020 by Eoin Brady
All rights reserved.

No part of this book may be reproduced in any form or by any electronic or mechanical means, including information storage and retrieval systems, without written permission from the author, except for the use of brief quotations in a book review.

This is a work of fiction. Names, characters, places and incidents are either the product of the author's imagination or are used fictitiously. Any resemblance to actual persons, living or dead, or locales is entirely coincidental

Published by Eoin Brady
Cover Design: Books Covered
Edited by Gheorghe Rusu

Printed in Dunstable, United Kingdom